Queen of Burlesque

Queen of Burlesque

The Autobiography of
YVETTE PARIS

PROMETHEUS BOOKS
BUFFALO, NEW YORK

94 93 92 91 90   5 4 3 2 1

Library of Congress Catalog Card Number 90–62764

ISBN 0-87975-639-X

Printed in the United States of America on acid-free paper.

To my loving husband, David March, who always gave me support,
for saying I could when everybody said I couldn't,
and to my children, who unselfishly shared their mother
with the exotic world for a while: "Mom loves you."

Contents

Foreword

Queen of Burlesque is one in a series of sexual autobiographies designed to allow the reader to learn about people whose lives are stigmatized by society because they engage in activities or occupations that society has labeled as sexual or not quite respectable. In a sense, these people do the kinds of things that many of us have fantasized about yet are fearful of doing ourselves. The popular image of such individuals is that they are depraved, drug-ridden people who lie, cheat, steal, and cannot be trusted under any circumstances. They have such overpowering sexual drives that everything in their lives is subordinated to their animalistic tendencies. Such beliefs, however, do not usually correspond to reality. Certainly Yvette Paris does not fit this stereotype.

Yvette Paris, born Barbara Ann Baker, is a professional in a field that a large percentage of the American public looks down upon. Yet she is a mother, a wife, a daughter, and a caring individual. How did she become a stripper? What was it like? How did she juggle her family life with her life as a burlesque queen in Times Square? These are some of the questions Yvette deals with honestly and unabashedly in her book. In describing her own story, she reveals insights into some larger aspects of human nature and the human condition. In a way, her life as a dancer and burlesque star totally contradicts what most of us imagine to be true of modern-day exotic dancers. She is probably not a typical example of today's dancers, but she grew to love the burlesque lifestyle as well as the family of people within the burlesque world who befriended and supported her along the way.

Yvette is slightly old-fashioned—not necessarily what we think of as a "liberated" woman. Indeed, you may be alarmed or surprised by her very nonfeminist response to some of the traumas she's suffered in her life. But unlike Marilyn Monroe, whom she greatly admires and often impersonates, Yvette is a strong, level-headed survivor, who operates on her own terms and within her own moral code. Her intelligence, vibrancy, and boldness—her warmhearted love of life— shine through in the pages of *Queen of Burlesque*.

Vern L. Bullough

Acknowledgments

I would like to thank the following people for their support in the making of this book: my dear husband, David March; my loving children, Jack Lambert and Juliet March; Veronica Vera for turning me on to Prometheus Books; Vern Bullough for sending my manuscript to Prometheus; Robert Basil of Prometheus for getting my book started; Kathleen Molik-Sarazin of Prometheus for getting the dust jacket together artistically; and Reg Gilbert, the editor in charge of my book, for taking the time to know me and keeping the book in my own words. Thank you, Jeanne O'Day, for my photo section, and thanks to my secretaries, Bea Lambert and Barbara Mazziotti. I must thank my fabulous photographers: James Kriegsmann, Jr., who shot the cover for my book, Gerasimos Livitsanos, Annie Sprinkle, James Lambert, Bill Swanson, David March, Niel Wexler, Dominique, Maurice Seymore, and many others. I would like to thank all the North Fourth Street people for the memories; my brother, Jack, for always being there when I needed him; and to Gramma: "Thanks for the Oly Cookin." I'd like to thank my dear friend Bob Rosen for taking me seriously and my Harmony Theatre pal Manny Rosen for his sense of humor and all his helpful ideas. I'd like to thank Bob Anthony, owner of the Harmony Theatre, for giving me the title of "Queen of Burlesque," this generation. Thank you, Ann Corio, for being my teacher and friend. A special thanks goes to the fabulous

Jennie Lee for putting me in the "Strippers Hall of Fame." Thank you, Dixie "Marilyn Monroe" Evans, for your burlesque stories. Thanks to all the girls I ever had a ball stripping with. Thanks to my fan club, for making me what I am today. Thank you, Patty and Herman, for being the best bosses in go-go and for having the only place I like to dance—Curtnicks. A special thanks to Joe "Call Me Tuesday" Franklin for helping me in show business, for writing the introduction to my book, and for just being my friend. In loving memory to my mom, Agnes Marie Baker, and my dad, Jacob Frank Baker, commonly known as "Westy." And thanks to me for having the balls to do all the shit in this book.

Introduction

Burlesque and vaudeville were the popular entertainment forms of a bygone era. Burlesque today is a term erroneously used to describe many exotic dance theaters, when in reality burlesque in its true form no longer exists. What exactly was burlesque? Burlesque meant variety and comedy. We got many of our best comedians from it, guys like Ed Wynn, Danny Thomas, Red Skelton, and Ol' Banjo Eyes himself, Eddie Cantor. Today, clips from Abbott and Costello's "Who's on First" are still breaking people up. "The Great One," Jackie Gleason, is now a cult figure with today's youth, proving that although the burlesque routines are old they are never stale. These comedians had timing and knew exactly how to get a laugh without resorting to obscenities. There's something about seeing Milton Berle in a dress that's so comical he doesn't even need to speak his lines—he can break up an audience with facial expressions alone.

From burlesque we also got some of the most beautiful and talented striptease artists in the business, ladies such as the great Ann Corio, Gypsy Rose Lee, Sherry Britton, and Margie Hart. These gals were masters of timing. They knew how to show an audience a lot—without showing too much! They were ladies in every aspect of the word and they never compromised their act. Burlesque was glamour, not raunch.

Today's dancers are very exotic and lovely. Most are very talented dancers, but they are not burlesque dancers. One would be hard pressed to find an actual burlesque dancer still performing today. There are no longer any comedians in today's burlesque, no more "top bananas," no more comedy skits—nothing. Burlesque as it was is dead.

One young lady that tried to keep burlesque glamorous and clean was a stripper named Yvette Paris. In today's stripping, where audiences are jaded and expect sexual and sometimes downright raunchy competition, there was Yvette with glamorous gowns, Sally Rand feather fans, and Ann Corio parasols. Yvette saw other girls killing themselves to please X-rated audiences, but she refused to compete. Instead she gave them a taste of what burlesque was really like and, much to her own surprise, became the favorite stripper of the New York circuit. Without employing anything off-color in her act and always conducting herself as a lady, Yvette went from being an underpaid go-go girl, to a "filler-in" stripper, to a "silver star" stripper, to a "golden star" stripper, and, finally, worked her way up to become the "Queen of Burlesque" in all of Times Square, a place that is not known for giving quarter to anyone.

Yvette became more and more famous for her old-time burlesque act. Through her dancing, Yvette saw and met many interesting and famous people. She experienced much in the exotic world. She observed many unfortunate events that happen to people who involve themselves in drugs and prostitution. Yvette decided she had a lot to say about the exotic world, so she wrote this book. When I first met Yvette, I asked her what her goal was. What did she want to achieve from this book? She told me that, apart from wanting to take a potshot at drugs, she wanted to help young girls who, after reading her book on the exotic world, might be discouraged from fantasizing about running away to the big city and living a life in the fast lane.

Yvette's book is fascinating. She gives a personal tour of the go-go bars, strip joints, peep shows, bachelor parties, and other aspects of the world of the exotic and erotic. While taking you into her own personal life at home with her family, she will also explode some of the myths about exotic people and tell you of the human beings inside them.

Yvette Paris is not a girl of the eighties—this is by self-admission. She is an old-fashioned girl with old-fashioned values. If she had performed back when burlesque was real burlesque, she would have been one of the all-time burlesque greats. But even though she came in at the tail end of burlesque, she still managed to make a name for herself, "Yvette Paris—The Queen of Burlesque." This persistent young lady will go far in life, and I'm proud to say that I gave her her first break in television on "The Joe Franklin Show." Miss Yvette Paris is "The Last Stripper."

Joe Franklin

Early Years

My father could have been wealthy had he chosen to be. Before he met my mother he owned three big homes. He was the head butcher for a large food chain, and he taught classes to young butchers on how to cut meat. On top of all that, he had his own business in Formica tabletops and furniture. He lost it all to drinking and gambling, though, so we never had a comfortable life. We always lived in slums and dreamed of better times. My mother used to tell me that someday I'd have my own bedroom, and in it there would be a white canopy bed with pink ruffles. I never got that bed. In fact, I never got my own room. I always had to sleep on the couch in the parlor. To this day I'm more comfortable sleeping on the couch.

Mom was one of six children. Her mother died when Mom was only nine years old, during the Great Depression. My grandfather could not take care of all those children and work too, so he put them in a Catholic home until they were older. My mother was the oldest of the girls. She hated the home. It was run by nuns and they were very strict. Eventually, they got out of the home, but my mother had to quit school to take care of the younger children. Her two older brothers went into the service, and her father worked hard in the weaving mills to support all of them.

When Mom was sixteen she worked as a maid for wealthy families and as a cook for priests—all this while she watched the younger children. She had no time for dating and other teenage activities. Every day, when her father came home hot and tired, he would bring two cans of beer, one in each pocket. One was for him and one was for her. It was the only thing she had to look forward to all day.

When Mom was twenty-nine she started dating a little. The kids were older, so she had more freedom. She was out on a date one night when a young man speeding along the highway hit the car she was in head-on. There were no seat belts in those days, so she went headfirst through the windshield. Her eye was out on her cheek, dangling from a nerve. Her forehead and a cheekbone were crushed in. For months after the accident she was picking glass out of her face. The pieces would surface in the form of whiteheads, then break through the skin, leaving her face scarred. Miraculously, her eye was saved, but her face was a mess. Plastic surgery was out of the question. She didn't have the money and the surgeons didn't have the knowledge they have today. She learned to live with her face, with the help of drinking.

Mom spent her nights bar hopping. She got into barroom brawls often. Once she beat up a British sailor for knocking America. My mother was an Amazon of a woman. She was of Irish background and loved a good fight, and, boy, could she hold her own. I inherited my Irish temper from her.

One night, while doing the rounds, Mom couldn't get the top button of her coat open for some queer reason. A man sitting next to her offered to assist her. He opened the coat for her. Enter, my father. Pop, or "Westy," as he liked to be called, had had a hard life, too. Pop grew up poor, the youngest of eight children. He became a Sunday school teacher and a choir boy. He fell in love with a nineteen-year-old beauty and they soon married. They had a lovely daughter and were very happy. War broke out and Pop went into the Army, leaving his young wife and baby behind with his mother.

While he was away, his wife stopped writing to him. When he came home after being gone for two years, she was pregnant by a sailor. Pop was heartbroken but took the baby in as his. He started over again with his young wife. Pop started working nights, but one evening he got sick and was sent home—only to find his wife in bed with another man. The marriage was over.

After a while, Pop got married again, this time to a nice Italian girl. She was twenty-eight years old. They would only be together a year. She developed cancer of the liver and died in Pop's arms. Before she died Pop watched her bite her bottom lip off in pain. Later he found out that she and a friend at the bank she worked in had embezzled thousands of dollars and were going to run away together. After that Pop walked into the nearest bar and told the bartender, "Set 'em up, and keep 'em coming." This was the first time he had ever done any drinking, but it would not be his last. Pop was thirty-five then and a card-carrying alcoholic by the time he was thirty-six.

Mom and Pop got married on the rebound. She had just broken up with her boyfriend, and Pop had just buried his wife. They knew each other only six months before they got married, but the marriage would last thirty years.

My mom's parents were of an Irish heritage that I don't know too much about. My great-grandparents were named Timothy and Jo Hannah O'Leary. They were nicknamed "The Fighting O'Learys," a family with red-hot tempers whose men drank a lot and whose women were always in church praying for the men's souls. Mom told me that great-grandfather O'Leary was walking home from the pub one day, carrying a pail of beer in one hand and his shillelagh (walking stick or cane) in the other, when a priest ran into him and dumped his pail of beer into the gutter. Ordinarily this would have been grounds for a good fist fight, but old Tim O'Leary kept his cool—a good Irishman will do anything to keep his name from being read in mass. Priests command much respect in Ireland.

Timothy's daughter was my mom's mother, Jo Hannah. At sixteen years old she married a German altar boy her own age named Frank Meisen in a Catholic church in America. Together they had six children. Mom was the fourth. My grandmother died at only twenty-nine from a kidney disease. Mom said her mother couldn't hold her water anymore, so there were newspapers strewn all over the floor, just like you have to do with a puppy. She had big black circles under her eyes.

When his wife died, Grandpa could not take care of all of his children and work at the same time, so he put them in a Catholic home, visiting them on weekends. Mom told me that a wealthy woman wanted to marry Grandpa, but she wasn't willing to take his children, so he never remarried. He once said, "No one could ever take your grandmother's place." During his life Grandpa suffered several heart attacks and at one point almost died from cancer, but he still lived to a ripe old age. One more heart attack finally proved fatal.

I never felt close to Grandpa. He wasn't the type to show physical love, although I'm sure he loved me. Whenever he came to visit us, I'd run up to him to give him a hug and a kiss. He would accept them coldly, then push me away. I hated his face. It had stiff, almost sharp, white stubble sticking out like cactus needles. I always tore up my face on them. Grandpa could always be counted on for money, though. He was always sending Mom money for rent, Christmas, and school clothes for me and my brother, Jack. He didn't like my father, who he thought was a bum who couldn't take care of his wife properly. I loved my father, but I must agree with Grandpa; my poor mother never had anything in her life. She died thinking her entire life was wasted.

My father's mother came from Amsterdam, Holland. Her maiden name was Annie Vanderwyde. She moved from Holland around the turn of the century to Holland, Michigan. She had five children from her first husband, John DeWitte. When he died, she married my grandfather, John Baker. From him she had three children, my Aunt Beatrice, Pop, and Frank, the baby of the family.

The DeWitte children never accepted the Baker children, and for years they hardly spoke. When Pop got married for the first time, the DeWittes didn't like his wife. They called his second wife, a nice Italian girl, a dirty Catholic. Mom, Pop's third wife, they called a dirty Irish Catholic. All of this family fighting upset Gramma terribly. She always wanted to keep peace with everyone, but it never worked.

Gramma was a hard-working woman, raising seven children and working in factories at the same time. Grandpa Baker couldn't do too much because he was crippled by a severe limp. He was also quite a *zip loppa* ("drinker" in Dutch). The burden was on Gramma's shoulders until her sons grew up and got jobs. The older boys worked in factories, and Pop got a job delivering telegrams for Western Union on his bike.

Gramma had a lot of sorrow in her life. One night it was pouring rain and Pop had a date. He didn't want to deliver telegrams that night and persuaded his seventeen-year-old kid brother, Frank, to take his route that night. He promised to fix the headlight on Frank's bike first thing in the morning if only Frank would work that night. Frank jumped at the chance to take Pop's route, just to get the light fixed. Uncle Frank wore a vinyl raincoat flapping in the breeze and sped off with Pop's telegrams in the pouring rain. By a cemetery in Totowa, New Jersey, a truck passed by Uncle Frank, caught his raincoat and dragged him for a mile before the coat tore loose. Uncle Frank was killed instantly, when his head hit the pavement.

When it got late and Frank didn't come home, Gramma and the rest of the family started to worry. After Pop got back from his date, there was a loud knock at the door. It was the police. They told Gramma that Frank was dead. Gramma had a breakdown. Pop, of course, felt to blame for sending his brother out in his place. I think Pop drank a lot because of that.

I was born, Barbara Ann Baker, in 1952. Two years later, Jack came along. Gramma was always good to me and Jack. She would always bring us a present when she came to visit, give us money to go to the store, and buy Dixie Cups for each of us, including the dog. When we moved to North Fourth Street, the place we lived the longest, during most of the 1960s, it was easy to visit her.

She lived near us in an apartment on a cobblestone road with Uncle Jim. Every morning in the summer I'd go up to visit Gramma. She was slightly hard of hearing so I never knocked on the door; I just walked in. (In those days, the early 1960s, people didn't have to lock their doors.) I had to walk up a steep hill, then go up a stairway and down a long, dark, cool hallway. The paint on the walls was shiny enamel forest green. You had to feel your way to Gramma's door.

Inside her apartment, it was sunny and gay. Gramma would be sitting in the parlor watching her soap operas, "The Guiding Light" and "Search for Tomorrow." Sometimes she would be asleep in her overstuffed easy chair. When I was younger and I found her sleeping, I'd wake her up and give her a big kiss. She was always glad to see me and got up right away to set the kitchen table by the window. She had plants on the fire escape outside the window. I used to admire them while Gramma fixed me either Dutch-style pancakes (deep-fried and sprinkled with sugar), waffles and syrup, or French toast. She always gave me a big tumbler of milk to wash down these terrific meals. Then she would fix herself a *bockie* (Dutch for coffee) and ask me all about school and how my art was coming along. It was common knowledge that one day I would become a famous artist—I come from a long line of excellent painters. Then Gramma would braid my hair and let me wear wooden shoes around the house. They hurt like hell!

Around Christmas I would come and show her my singing skills for the Christmas pageant. I sang her every carol I knew (which was a lot) and she loved it. When it was around Christmas Gramma always made a Dutch doughnut called *oly bollen*. Gramma made the doughnuts for the whole family. She would be in the kitchen for hours standing over a deep pot bubbling with hot lard, dropping in little balls of dough with raisins. She'd remove them with a slotted spoon and drain them on brown paper bags lined with sugar. When she was making this Christmas treat, you could smell it all the way down the street. Gramma's sisters and daughters tried to make the doughnuts but never got the hang of it. I can make them, just like Gramma, though, and I do every Christmas to keep Gramma's memory alive.

Uncle Jim died from throat cancer in 1966. He lived with Gramma and never married. He took very good care of her. Uncle Jimmy was a conductor on the Erie Railroad. When he died, Gramma got a hefty pension, plus insurance. Uncle Jimmy's death left her a wreck. She was afraid to stay in the apartment alone. She said she saw the ghost of her Jimmy walking around. As long as I could remember, Gramma had talked to the dead. She would speak Dutch every night in her bedroom before she went to sleep. She told me she was talking to her loved ones. I inherited a similar habit from Gramma. I talk to the dead almost every night in my sleep.

Gramma got so afraid of being alone that she often asked me to sleep over. I was a child and afraid of seeing Uncle Jimmy's ghost, so I declined. All of Gramma's children, except Pop, had spare rooms in their houses, but none of them offered to take her in to live with them. Their children were all married and living in other parts of the country, but they wouldn't take Gramma in. Pop offered to let Gramma live with us. It would be cramped, but Pop believed in taking in family and making room. Unfortunately, Pop was the youngest son, and by Dutch custom the oldest son is the head of the family when the father is dead. All decisions on Gramma's fate were in the hands of Uncle John. He and all of Gramma's children, except Pop, felt it best for Gramma to be placed in a home for the elderly. Pop and I were dead set against it, but Gramma respected the wishes of the oldest male and went to live in the Holland Home. But her children betrayed her. They took all her insurance and pension money and took a fabulous trip to Holland. They never asked Gramma if maybe she wanted to visit the old country. I visited Gramma in the home as much as I could. I was only sixteen and had no car, and, when I asked Pop to take me, he refused. Gramma was always hollering about his drinking, and he didn't want to hear it, so we visited her less and less.

One day, when I was sixteen, I decided to go visit Gramma by myself. It was mid-July, ninety-eight degrees, and the home was ten miles away. I am a fainter. I keel over in the heat. Halfway to the home I started to get dizzy and nauseated, but I plodded on. Then my sandals started cutting my feet. Finally, they fell apart, and I walked the rest of the way barefoot on hot, gravelly, country sidewalks. Sweat was pouring into my eyes, burning them and blurring my vision. When I got to the home, my feet were bleeding and my face was sunburned. When Gramma saw me, she rushed me to the cafeteria and got me a cold Seven-Up. Although she was very happy to see me, she wished I hadn't walked all the way up in the heat. I stayed for a while and kept her company, but soon I had to go. When I got back to North Fourth Street, I collapsed on the living room floor. When I woke up, Mom was putting cold washcloths on my forehead.

Once in 1970 I took a bus up to the home and signed Gramma out for the day. Together we took the bus downtown, where I treated her to a major shopping spree. First we had lunch in her favorite restaurant. Then we went to buy a hat—she loved hats. She couldn't make up her mind which she liked better, the navy blue one with the veil or the gray one with the pale pink flowers. We got them both. Then she needed a nightlight, so we got a fancy one with a soft pink bulb. We got her some crocheting supplies and some plain handkerchiefs, which she called "hankies," to crochet colored lace on. Finally, we got a corset, stockings, a plant, and a fancy tea kettle. Then I brought her to my house and treated everyone to a huge pizza dinner. She loved pizza. She called it a "bitz." Later Pop and I took her home. She was so happy with her loot, just like a big kid.

Gramma started to get senile. Her doctors told us she was drifting further and further into the past from loneliness and a broken heart because her kids never came to visit her anymore. She didn't even know me when I went to visit her after I married for the first time. At first she thought I was one of the kids in the Christmas pageant that was entertaining the old people that night. Then she started calling me Jackie, mixing me up with my brother. Jack never went to see her. One day in 1972, Mom called me up and said Gramma had died in her sleep. I put down the phone and sat on the couch and cried my heart out.

Rumor has it that Pop was not my father. Supposedly Mom got pregnant by an Italian or Irish guy, and Pop felt sorry for her and married her. I don't really know and I don't really care. I only know one father, such as he was, and I loved him, but to this day I'm not sure he loved me. This feeling dates from an incident that happened when I was about five years old. Mom and Pop took my brother and me to a castle overlooking the city. There was a stone wall on a balcony that we stood on as we spied the city through a pay telescope. I remember my mother holding my baby brother some distance from the wall. I was with Pop, who had me on his shoulders. He was pointing out parts of the city. It was a cold and very windy day. Suddenly, Pop stood me on the wall and walked away! The drop over the stone wall was terrible, with jagged rocks and smashed beer bottles at the bottom. I stood like a statue, petrified, hands stiffly at my sides. Tears streamed down my cheeks and urine ran warm down my legs. I could feel it in my socks. The wind whipped my face, and, as I tried to call "Daddy," it took my breath away. In the background I could hear Mommy and Daddy arguing. She wanted me taken down, but Pop told her to *shut up*. After an eternity, Mom ran up and grabbed my tiny, frozen, statue body off the ledge. She took me to where she'd been sitting and tried to calm me down. I was sobbing. The urine-soaked socks were now cold and chafing my ankles. All Pop did was shake his head and mumble swear words at my mother. Mom had a bag of jelly doughnuts with her and she gave me one. I noticed little criss-crosses on the bottom of the doughnut. Mom was smoking and some ashes fell on it. She dusted them off but I was grossed out and couldn't eat the doughnut.

Today I sometimes visit that balcony. I stand by the stone wall and look over at the rocks below. It's still a steep, ugly drop, and the wind still blows strongly up there. Maybe Pop was just trying to make me into the boy he had wanted. He had terrorized me the year before, just as senselessly. He was working in the meat department at the Grand Union supermarket, and one day he brought me into the store. I was sitting in the shopping cart, and Pop wheeled me into the back where the butchers cut up meat. It was very cold. Then Pop put a huge, live lobster into the shopping cart with me. I froze solid as this slimy thing from the deep crawled closer, clacking its claws at me. Just then a lady butcher came out; she must have been shocked at what she saw because she grabbed the lobster out of the cart and then ranked Pop out something fierce. When he got home, Mom gave it to him, too.

After Mommy died I looked Pop in the eye and asked him why he stood me on that wall. Surely he knew that if I fell I would have been killed instantly. In a second I was sorry I asked that question. Pop went pale gray and his mouth hung open but no words came out.

Pop is long dead now and the reason went with him, but I was never sure of his love for the rest of my life. I used to think perhaps it was because I wasn't really his child, or maybe that he had me insured and would come into a lot of money at my death. But what puzzles me the most is how my mother let it go on for even one second. These are mysteries I must live with. It's ancient history and I have to put it to sleep.

As a toddler, my biggest fear was that my mother would die or leave me. One day she did leave me. I was three years old. I went wild with hysterics. My dad was taking care of me. Poor Pop tried everything in his power to calm me down. He called me "square mouth," because of all my crying. I wanted my mother! Pop made us a nice dinner. He was an excellent cook, but then he should have been—he was the sergeant of the mess hall when he was in the Army. He made doughnuts. I remember he cut them out with a glass, then made the hole with a shot glass. They were good! Later we watched television for awhile, then we went to bed. I slept with Pop that night. First he amused me by playing a game called "Catch the Ticket." We had one of those old, heavy, wooden 1950s beds. It had a reading light hanging over the backboard. Pop had a purple movie ticket stub that I was supposed to try to catch, only he was too fast for me. I laughed so hard I got the hiccups. Pop gave me a large tumbler of water, then I fell fast alseep. The next morning poor Pop was soaked. I'd wet the bed.

That afternoon there was a knock on the door. It was my aunt and uncle. Mom was back! In her arms was something in a blue blanket.

It was "him"—my baby brother. Everyone made such a fuss over him. I was allowed to see him, but I couldn't touch him or breathe on him. I have to admit, he sure was cute. He was chubby with curious blonde ringlets all over his head. He had deep blue eyes and rosy cheeks. The cutest part about him was his large, soft Dumbo ears.

Pop seemed to forget all about me. I found the purple ticket stub and brought it to him to play Catch the Ticket, but he sent me away. As the days passed by I got more and more jealous of baby Jack. I felt totally ignored, and I was. Pop had always wanted a son. Mom told me he'd been disappointed when I was born, so much so that he called me Bobbi instead of Barbara Ann. My mother started finding little teeth marks on Jack. They were mine. I would bite him, pinch him, and try to pull his ringlets off. I stopped when Mom caught me one day and warmed my ass.

When Jack was about two years old, he became very skinny and pale. He looked sickly, but otherwise he seemed healthy. My grandmother was from Holland, and, like most Europeans, she thought a baby was unhealthy if it wasn't fat. She would scare the hell out of all of us by saying, "Poor little Yoppie, he's going to die." "Yoppie" was her nickname for my father, therefore my brother was "little Yoppie." I was sad. As much as I thought my brother was a crumb, I still didn't want him to die. I put my jealousy aside and became very protective of Jack. We became very close. At one time we were the only friends each other had, but that was O.K. We got along fine. There was only a three-year age difference.

Pop didn't believe in doctors. When I was six years old, I developed "Scarlet Tina," a painful sore throat and a very high fever that made me red all over, hence the "scarlet." I had this dreaded fever for almost a week. Mom kept me in bed. I was delirious. I heard her begging Pop to take me to the doctor, but he refused. He said I just had a cold and it had to run its course. A huge fight broke out between them. Mom was throwing pots and pans at Pop. I could hear it all but I was too weak to move. Jack crept into my parents' bedroom, where I was lying all bundled up. He called me sissy— he was scared of their fighting. I don't blame him, so was I. Jack sat in the corner like a mouse, leaning against the heavy oak dresser. He was trembling.

Mom won the battle. Next thing I knew she dressed me to the teeth. It was cold out, so on went my leggings, woolen hat, scarf, heavy coat, and mittens on a string that ran up the sleeve of my coat, across my neck, and down the other sleeve, so I wouldn't lose them. I stood there unable to move, I had so many clothes on.

After the doctor examined me, he gave me a needle. Then, as Mom was getting me dressed like Nanook of the North again, we could hear the doctor ranking Pop out for not getting me to him sooner. Then he told my mother, "If you had let her go one more day, she would have died." All hell broke loose in the car on the way home. Mom was hotter than the devil's butt, and Pop knew enough not to fight back. He knew she was right.

I still had to stay in bed, but I was feeling much better. My throat was still sore. I could hear the family having the after-dinner ritual of ice cream and walnut topping. I was not allowed to have ice cream. Mom said it would cause phlegm. I could suck on an ice cube, though. I could hear bowls clattering, someone dropping a spoon, and my mom saying "company's coming." She said that every time a spoon dropped.

When the family wasn't looking, engrossed in the "Red Skelton Show," Jack came to the bedroom to see me. He was a sight. Jack had a peculiar habit of stirring up his ice cream until it was so soft it was almost liquid. He ate only chocolate ice cream, so he had a chocolate mustache. There he stood, in his bathrobe and Donald Duck slippers, stirring madly at his bowl of ice cream. Finally, he came over and gave me some of his ice cream soup. Boy, did it taste good. He was lucky he didn't catch my sore throat.

Jack was a very shy kid. He liked to stay home and play with his police cars and fire engines. If you asked him what he wanted to be when he grew up, he would never hedge. "I want to be a cop," he always said. We all thought that was cute, but he was very serious about it. I was going to be a ballerina. Jack would get a pat on the head from the grownups, and I would get a wisenheimer crack about my chubby thighs.

We did a lot of bar hopping with my parents. We hated it. Almost every night we'd be in some bar, sitting in a booth, eating potato chips and oyster crackers while Mom and Pop got crocked. I became an expert on the songs that played on the jukebox. Pop was going through his hocking phase. He would load up a wagon with anything in the house of value, like the toaster, the television set, and Mom's wedding ring, take it down to old Gotlieb, and hock it all for a few bucks for bar hopping.

We used to always do bar hopping on Halloween because the money was good. We kids would walk up and down the bar with our trick-or-treat bags open and beg for money. When we had fleeced the bar people for all we could, we would go back to Pop at the booth and turn over our loot to him for more drinks. One Halloween I made friends with a barmaid. I liked her because she told me I was pretty. Suddenly, a man in a hideous witch mask ran behind the bar and grabbed her. She played along with the guy, acting scared and screaming. It was her husband, and everybody knew but me. I started screaming and crying because the pretty lady was being killed by a Halloween witch. It took a lot on her husband's part to convince me that he was only kidding. Finally, he was able to buy me off with a bag of cheese doodles. After that incident, Mom used to tell me, if I got out of bed at night, a witch that looked just like that would come and grab me and take me crashing through the window, and fly away with me on her broomstick, boil me in a big pot, and eat me. She told me that story because I was a wanderer. I would get bored at night and roam all over the house, getting into mischief. But after Mom told me that story, I was afraid to leave my bed—and I started bed-wetting. Every time it thundered, I was afraid the old witch was outside my window waiting for me. I was broken of my bed-wetting one day when Pop rubbed my pissy pants in my face. I never did it again.

We visited Gramma a lot at this time. I loved to go to her house. She always had a present for me and Jack. Later I found out Pop was only going to visit her to borrow money. Mom had to beg my

Uncle Jim (Pop's brother, who still lived at home) for money for
food. Uncle Jim gave her the money, but he was pissed off at Pop
for being such a lousy provider.

Pop got a job driving a truck for the Salvation Army. Almost
every day he would bring home industrial barrels full of toys. Some
were broken, but not too badly. Once Jack got a milk truck with
three wheels that gave him endless hours of fun, and I got a big
rag doll with a dented-in, plastic face. I can still see my mother with
a big hat pin picking the dents out. The doll ended up looking pretty
good, if you didn't mind pinholes. I pretended they were freckles.
Jack and I waited expectantly for Pop to come home every day.
He never came home empty-handed.

One Christmas we were in exceptionally bad shape financially.
We couldn't even afford a Christmas tree. I used to listen to Mom
and Pop talking at night in the kitchen when I was supposed to
be sleeping. This time they were talking about Christmas. Pop felt
terrible that we couldn't even afford a tree. Mom was near tears.
A couple of days before Christmas, I watched my mom from the
warm kitchen window out in the backyard breaking long branches
off a peach tree. It was very cold and windy. Her dress was blowing
all over the place. She pushed wisps of her black hair from her face
as she struggled with the peach tree. I couldn't imagine what she
was doing.

When she came in, her lips were purple from the cold. She brought
out our Christmas decorations box, took an end table, and wrapped
chimney wrapping paper around it. Next, she took a large vase and
arranged the peach branches. Then she draped our blue Christmas
lights all over them. She took a box of Red Cross cotton, pulled
it off into cotton balls, and put the balls all over the branches to
look like snow. When she finished, Jack and I were puzzled. The
thing looked strangely pretty—not exactly like a Christmas tree, but
not exactly unlike one, either. When Mom turned the lights out,
it really was beautiful. The whole room glowed in a soft blue light.

Christmas dinner was hamburgers and mashed potatoes. Our
presents came from the Salvation Army, and we had lots of them

because people gave away a lot of toys around Christmas to make room for new toys. Despite Mom and Pop's worries, it was a Christmas to remember.

My brother was my only friend in school and vice versa. He was very shy and withdrawn, and I didn't make friends very easily because I was too much of a tomboy, so we were very close. Because Jack was so little and skinny, he was picked on constantly. The kids were very cruel to him. They teased him unmercifully about his big ears. My brother was always getting beaten up after school. Being his older sister and quite a good scrapper, I would fight his fights for him. Often we would run home together to avoid the school bullies.

Once I was sick and had to stay home, so Jack had to go to school by himself. It was winter and very cold. Mom had Jack all bundled up, wearing a long, off-white, silk scarf that hung down his back. Two big bullies chased my brother for three blocks before they caught up with him. When they got him, they punched the hell out of him, dragged him into a backyard, and tried to hang him by his scarf from a tree branch.

One of the neighborhood kids tore over to our house to tell my mother. "They're trying to kill Jackie!" I was lying on the couch in my pajamas watching cartoons when he came in. That was it! I flew into a rage, jumped into my clothes and shoes, forgot about my coat and my cold, and ran like the devil himself to my brother's defense. What I saw when I got there still makes my eyes water. My brother was hanging from a tree branch by his scarf, which was tied tight around his neck. One of the boys was trying to hoist my brother up by the scarf. Both of them had plastic baseball bats they were using to hit him with. Tears streamed down Jack's little face, which was turning purple. His ears were blood red and so was my God-awful temper. I found a board with nails in it lying in a pile of debris by a shed, and I went berserk pounding the daylights out of both bullies. I opened a lip, lacerated an eye, and, finally, just before my mom got there to pull me off those monsters, whacked one kid in the forehead, splitting it down the middle. He had to get stitches. Later that night the kid's parents came to the door to demand that Mom and Pop pay for his stitches. All hell broke loose. Mom chased them off the porch and down the street. They never bothered us again.

My brother took a lot of shoving around until he was about twelve years old. Then something happened. He finally snapped. He started fighting back, and soon he was bullying the bullies. He grew tough and mean. He was an excellent street fighter, and no one got in Jack Baker's way. He started fighting *my* battles.

Unfortunately, as teenagers we went our separate ways. I never knew what he was up to, and he never knew what I was doing. We met at the dinner table, then went off to our own worlds. The only things we had in common were our mutual love for Mom and Pop and our mutual hate for poverty. We both vowed to break away from being poor some day. Jack went on to marry a beautiful girl he'd loved since he was fifteen. They have three wonderful children. He realized his dream to become a police officer and has gotten many awards for bravery. I'm proud of him.

Things went from bad to worse, and, in 1958, we moved to a much poorer neighborhood. There was lots of racial tension. Pop was driving a bakery truck and had to work nights, leaving Mom and us alone. Mom never slept. She sat up until four in the morning, when Pop got done. He didn't knock on the door. Prowlers at that time used that ploy. Instead, he kicked the door three times hard, so Mom would know it was him. The local prowlers got wind of this and tried kicking on our door one night when Pop was working— only it was about midnight, not four in the morning. Mom was scared. She made me and Jack hide in a closet while she got one of Pop's huge butcher knives and went to the door, where she yelled for my father, "Jake, there's a prowler at the door, get your gun!" It worked. She heard footsteps running down the hall. After that, Mom sat up every night with the butcher knife on her lap and wouldn't even doze off. Another time, while she was watching television, she saw two hands slowly lift up the parlor window. We were on the first floor. She slowly got up and let out the loudest, most blood-curdling scream I had ever heard. The prowler ran away. Mom was a brave woman. I often wonder what would have happened if she had let herself sleep.

Right around this time, Pop's gangster friends would come around for money he owed them. Mom and Jackie and I were under threat by the loan-shark strong-arm men—if Pop didn't pay up, Mom's face would be busted, along with our little arms.

Sex was never mentioned in my family except when someone said "fuck you." Talk about sex was taboo. My mother and father never slept together, at least not that I ever saw. For years I slept with my mother, and my brother slept with my father. I know my father was a horny little devil, but my mother was a prude, thus forcing Pop into the arms of other women, porno movies, and massive masturbation.

Once Pop came back from a porno flick earlier than usual. He was very pissed off. He told us he was thrown out of the movie because he was wearing shorts. He failed to tell us the shorts were down to his knees, and he was doing something he shouldn't have been doing in public!

As a child I had my first brush with the forbidden subject when I discovered Pop's "picnic basket of porn." This was a typical wooden picnic basket that contained not only spiders but a number of de-lightful little pulpy books that reeked of mildew. Smut paperbacks! On the covers were artistic naked and semi-naked ladies, and on the inside were the steamiest stories that ever turned a little girl's face red.

I'd sneak into the hall closet that contained Pop's overcoats and shirts. One day I discovered smudgy, black-and-white photos of not-very-attractive women, fat as hell, in Pop's overcoat pockets. Come to think of it, Pop had more overcoats than the average man. I'd very quietly open the picnic basket of porn and read pure smut by flashlight. I loved it. In time I'd circle the parts I liked best, then reread them. The basket also contained *Playboy* magazines and a deck of French playing cards with women who looked like they wore black lipstick. I'd open the *Playboys* and stare in wonderment at the big-breasted ladies gracing the pages. Then I'd feel where my breasts would be someday, but for now they were only on order. I'd think, "Will I ever look that beautiful?" I wanted to pose like they did, on shiny satin. Then I'd look at the men and women posing on the playing cards. I didn't know what they were doing, but I'd feel my face flush. I was excited, but I wasn't quite sure why. These trips to the closet ended one day. I came home from school to discover that Mom had cleaned out the picnic basket and replaced Pop's stash with *Readers Digests*! How sad. This was the end of an era. I was only seven.

I was in the middle of a math test in the sixth grade when President Kennedy was shot. We were dismissed from school immediately. When I got home, Pop was watching the recaps on television. It was pretty shocking. I never saw anyone killed on television before. I think what bothered me most was seeing the president alive and waving to the crowds one minute, then covered with blood and dying the next. I kept thinking that when he was taking a shower that morning he had no idea that he would soon be dead. I tried to put myself in Jackie Kennedy's place, his blood splashed on her. I shudder to think how she must have felt.

Pop was a very prejudiced man. Even though the television coverage shocked him, he couldn't wait to get in a racist crack. He said to us, "I'm not surprised he was killed. Nobody likes a nigger lover and that's what Kennedy was. Look at the last president who was a nigger lover. Too bad he wasn't killed before he set all the slaves free. It's his fault that the niggers are so surly today."

This kind of talk was like fingernails scratching on a blackboard to me. I never inherited Pop's blind hatred of all nonwhite races. I reminded Pop that his own people, the Dutch, were partly responsible for bringing the slaves over to America in the first place. They didn't want to come over here.

I was the undisputed black sheep of my family, mostly because

I wouldn't accept their prejudiced way of thinking. They put down everybody—blacks, Jews, Puerto Ricans, Poles, Scots, Irish, Germans, even the English. My father and brother were the main culprits. My mother really just went along with whatever the male lead was. My father's biggest worry when he was going to die was, "Don't bury me next to a jig."

Still, it's not only the white people who are prejudiced. Black people are often guilty, too. They are still blaming white people for slavery. If you read the history books, you will find that some black native chiefs sold their own people into slavery. Besides, slavery is ancient history. None of today's blacks were ever slaves, and none of today's whites were ever slave traders.

My family called me a "nigger lover" because I refused to join in their insipid conversations around the dinner table. So I ate in the parlor.

Not long after President Kennedy was killed, the Beatles hit the United States. I was all of twelve. My girlfriend Sally and I were just as crazy as the people you see in all the flim clips from documentaries on the group. We screamed and cried whenever we saw the Beatles on television. When we heard them sing on the radio, we went radio silent and drooled over the fantastic love songs. The week before they actually came to the States, we were inundated with Beatles collectibles. My friends and I had Beatles looseleaf notebooks, Beatles boots, Beatles wigs, Beatles dolls, Beatles t-shirts, and Beatles cards. We carried our cards around in a shoe box. A pack of Beatles cards cost us a nickel. You got five colored cards of the Beatles and a piece of stale pink bubble gum that tasted like soap. The very first cards were black and white.

It was a Sunday night the first time the Beatles performed on the "Ed Sullivan Show." My girlfriend Sally and I glued ourselves to the set and waited impatiently for the other acts to get off. As a performer myself, I can now say that I feel sorry for the people who went on before the Beatles that night. They went totally unappreciated. The producers knew exactly what they were doing by making the Beatles the last act. Excitement had built up to such an extent in both the audience at the studio and the audience at home that, when the Beatles were finally introduced, all hell broke loose. My girlfriend and I started screaming and crying, pulling on each other's pajamas. To this day I don't really know what made us act so crazy. Even now, when I see a film clip of the Beatles in their very early years, I still get excited and feel crazy inside.

I had it all planned out that I was going to marry Paul, and my girlfriend was going to marry George. We sat around for hours making elaborate plans on how we were going to meet them. The main problem on our minds was what we would do when we finally captured our favorite Beatles. We knew we were too young for grown-up stuff like doing you know what, or even kissing, so we decided that the Beatles would be happy just to sing to us until we grew up and could do you know what. I knew this was true because of their song "I'm So Happy Just to Dance with You."

For a lot of my childhood, we were a family on the go. I first lived with my mother in an apartment with her father in Paterson, New Jersey. Mom left Pop for a few weeks immediately after my birth, because Pop was accusing her of being a ginny whore, saying that the baby wasn't his but some guy named Joe's. Mom used to go with Joe at the same time she was going with Pop.

Next we lived in a home Pop owned in Hawthorne, New Jersey. I remember it vaguely. We had prize tulips and jumbo tomatoes—Pop had a green thumb. Once he even got a prize for a very large lettuce. He invented a new strain of tulip by cutting slits into the bulbs, and pouring food coloring into them. He got beautiful multi-colored tulips as a result, and there was a write-up about him and his tulips in the papers. We had chickens and fresh eggs every morning, too. One day the chickens got out and flew all over Lincoln Avenue, a very busy street. I watched from the window as Mom and her friend Myrtle chased the chickens with brooms back into the coop. Mom was terrified of them. I laughed so hard that I peed myself, but I never moved away from the window. I just stood in a puddle of pee. Poor mom, after she came in to rest from chicken chasing, she had to get me cleaned up. The work never ended for her. Next we moved to Van Houten Street in Paterson. We had a pretty big backyard with a small hill in it. Across the street was a Victorian-style funeral parlor. It looked very sinister. Mom told me there was an old witch who lived there, and, if I ever wandered away from the house, she would get me. Today I sometimes go past that same funeral parlor, and I still get a little shiver from it. My brother was born while we lived at the Van Houten house.

When I was six we moved to a bad section of town not too far away. It was a tenement building on Auburn Street. The place was dangerous. There was a lot of racial tension in the building. This is where my mother stayed awake all night when Pop was working late and where I started school at the Seventh Day Adventist Church. Mom used to walk me all the way to school every morning, quite a distance, then be waiting for me after school. She was terrified, but she never left me alone. Mom was smart, and she quickly made friends with several of the black women in the neighborhod, so after a while she was less on edge.

One day, while coming to pick me up at school, three big, black teens shoved her against a fence and threatened to beat her senseless unless she gave them all her money. Mom only had about fifty cents to buy me an ice cream and a coloring book (she always bought me a little something every day after school), so she gave the youths the fifty cents. They slapped her in the head and left. She was very late that day picking me up, and I was scared standing all alone in the playground waiting for her. She kept the incident from me as best she could. On the way home we saw the good Adventists ride right by us, tooting the horn and waving, but they didn't like Mom because she was pretty and painted her face like a Jezebel and wanted no part of Bible meetings. Some Christians! Mom had said that she tripped and fell and the money for my coloring book went down the sewer, but that night she broke down crying when Pop came home and told him what really happened. She thought I was asleep, but I heard every word.

The next day Mom called the minister of the church and told him what happened. He was very nice and offered to have me picked me up in the morning and dropped off after school. So now I had to ride with a God-fearin' church woman and her daughter, both mean as hell. They read from the Bible at every red light and made me recite psalms until I was dry in the mouth. They said it was the only way to cleanse a devil baby. They had me slated to be a missionary in the Congo. The big dream of all these Adventist kids and their parents was to become missionaries. I would make a splendid missionary once I broke away from my mother, the "evil one," they called her.

Soon we moved again, to a lovely town called People's Park. We were very happy there. The backyard was grassy, with a tree. And the bathroom had a modern, triangular, pink tub. I had never seen anything but the old-fashioned cat's-paw tubs. It made me want to take a bath right away. The kitchen was painted blue with blue cabinets. I loved the linoleum, shiny blue starbursts with gold glitter sprinkled all over it. This was the Ritz!

We had to move the very next week. The person who'd rented us the apartment had no authority to do so, and the real landlord wanted us out. I was heartbroken. We moved to a town called Prospect Park. It was also very nice, with quiet, tree-lined streets and the Dutch influence everywhere. The school was very good and just around the corner from my house. Our backyard had a red maple tree in the middle of it. I met my favorite animal, Tommy Cat, there and had plenty of woods to explore with my new friends. In spite of all my fun, I was at my most sickly in Prospect Park. I was dreadfully anemic and suffered from nosebleeds so massive I would almost go into shock.

I was watching the "Flintstones" after school the first time it happened. All of a sudden, I started choking on my own blood. I sat up, and the blood just poured out in buckets. Towels were soaked with blood, one after the other. By the time Pop came home at five, I was going into shock. Mom had me bundled up in blankets, but I was still freezing to the point that my teeth were actually chattering. Pop tried to stop the bleeding by shoving a piece of orange peel under my top lip and pressing it into my nose, but it did no good. His hand was forced. I was rushed to the hospital in an ambulance. The doctors cauterized my nose and diagnosed me as being severely anemic. I was put on a strong iron and vitamin regimen (liquid, I couldn't swallow pills), and told never to pick my nose. The tissue inside my nose was as thin as toilet paper. The least little thing and I'd be back in the hospital. I was scared because I never knew when it would happen again. My biggest fear was that it would happen in school.

At Prospect Park we looked forward to Pop coming home from work every night around five or six P.M. He worked in an Army/Navy store downtown. Every day on his break he would go to the five-and-ten and pick up a little something for me and Jack. The first thing we would do when Pop got home was rush him. "What's in the bag, what's in the bag?" Pop would produce Monkey Sticks or coloring books and crayons. One day he started a collection for us. Every night he would bring home, carefully wrapped in tissue, a little knick-knack made of glass and painted. One night he brought two glass birds. I got a pink-crested bird, and Jackie got a pale blue parakeet. The next night it was dogs. I got a white French poodle, and Jackie got a boxer. The suspense of it!

In 1962 we moved to North Fourth Street—just an ordinary street of row houses. It was no slum or ghetto, but, of course, it was not a place millionaires went to play, either. It was a magical place that was there for only one decade, the 1960s, and then disappeared. The street is still there but it was the people that made it magical, and they are all gone. Several of the families there really merged into something like one big family, like all the kids were brothers and sisters and we all had many mothers and fathers. It was all over like the stage play *Brigadoon*. I can bring North Fourth Street back for a little while whenever I run into any of the North Fourth Street people.

The kids in our neighborhood did things as a group. We'd all share the holidays, like Halloween, which was something we planned for months in advance. Come trick-or-treat, we'd stay out until eleven at night, then come home and compare our loot. Times were simpler then. It never occurred to us that someone might poison the candy or put razor blades in the apples. We would eat our candy as we went along. There was no such thing as having it X-rayed at the hospital.

Christmas was magical! After waking up early to tear through our gifts, we would go visit our friends to see what they got, and the rest of the day was spent going from house to house, eating Christmas candy and drinking ginger ale. One Christmas my mother made herself sick when she and Pop walked two miles in the snow to get me a doll I just had to have. My mother didn't have boots and she was bare-legged. The slushy snow covered her cheap cloth loafers. "Thanks, Mom."

The houses on North Fourth Street would try to outdo each other in Christmas lights. I loved the way the whole street glowed in warm colors while the snow drifted down silently. Every year I was in a Christmas pageant at the school. I would start practicing my carols right after Thanksgiving. One year I had a solo spot. Because I could hit the high notes at the time, I was given the song "Oh Holy Night" to sing. Pop was drinking at the time, but that didn't stop him from coming to see my solo at the pageant. After my performance, I went back to my seat, and all was quiet in the huge auditorium. Then, to my horror, my father rose and started singing "Old King Wrinkled Ass," his version of "Good King Wenceslaus." Talk about dying from embarrassment.

On our street all the parents had open house for New Year's Eve. The kids would travel from house to house eating and catching glimpses of Guy Lombardo on the tube (all our parents had him on). We'd drink ginger ale and pretend it was champagne. The fathers got hordes of firecrackers ready for when the new year rolled in. Around midnight we all made sure we were in one place for the big countdown. "Happy New Year!" The kids ran out into the cold night banging pots and pans and throwing iceballs. The fathers blew up the sidewalks with Black Cat firecrackers and everyone hugged and kissed.

On Easter, we all got dressed up in new clothes. It was the only time we looked neat and the only time my brother and I got anything new to wear. We'd all walk around and take pictures of each other. Then, we heathens would walk up the hill to any church at random and pretend to be interested in the sermon. Afterwards, we'd walk home, eat ham, get changed, and go out and hop fences. My mother would then put our "good" clothes away for the next high state occasion.

Hopping fences was a North Fourth Street pastime. All the kids on the block often did it together, and we had great fun trying to move so fast that we didn't get caught by the neighbors, who naturally didn't go for the idea of a pack of kids stomping over their tomato patches. We would start up at one end of the street and work our way all the way down to the other end. Hopping fences was good therapy for us. If you got chewed out by your parents, you could go hop fences and get it out of your system. Underneath part of the street were old barns where horses used to be kept. We called them "the caves." Going to the caves was an adventure. There were bats, rats, and ghosts in the caves, but we never saw any.

It was too hot to stay inside during the summer, so we would all stay out front of the house until pretty late at night. It was quite safe. The parents would be out there, too. Everyone seemed to congregate in front of our house. We had the pale blue street light shining down on us, and we also had "the wall." Everyone sat on our wall. It was made of cold stone, so it was nice to park your can on it when it was hot. We'd wait for the ice cream truck to come by ringing jingle bells or for the truck that went by with a ride on the back, like the Whip or the Flying Cages.

Twice we had a block dance. We sealed off the street with sawhorses, someone donated a jukebox, and the mayor came down with free ice cream. All the mothers made salads and cakes. The liquor store sent over free cases of soda, and the community newspaper took pictures. My brother and I won a twist contest, and Jack also won the Limbo Rock contest. No one else was that flexible. We had spotlight dancing and line dances. The music was all 1950s and early 1960s—but then this was 1962!

Summer was a time for ghost stories and visiting graveyards, looking for Annie's ghost. Annie was a girl who supposedly lost her baby so she drowned herself in a river. People said you could see Annie walking the cemeteries at night, looking for her baby. We never did. When we weren't traipsing through graveyards, we had all-night double-dutch marathons or played Monopoly for money.

My mom dressed like this, every day, except for funerals: a baggy floral housedress covered by a full-length paisley apron with a large clump of safety pins hanging off the strap of the apron ("You never know when you'll need a pin," she'd say), and a checkered dish towel hanging from one shoulder at all times; flip-flop fuzzy pink or blue slippers, no stockings; hair tied back in a short ponytail with a stylish loose strand hanging down her forehead; and a cigarette dangling from her mouth at all times, removed only to shout an obscenity at me, my brother, or Pop. Pop always dropped his laundry as soon as he got in the house. He would strip down to shit-stained baggy boxer shorts with little, old-fashioned cars all over them. He refused to ever bathe.

I was thirteen years old the first time I was kissed. I had been watching "Batman" with a really handsome sixteen-year-old boy. I had the biggest crush on him, and I was pretty sure he liked me, too. After the show I walked him to the door. Out in the pitch-black hallway, he grabbed me and pressed a hard French kiss on me. Since I had never kissed a boy before, I had no idea you were supposed to open your mouth. I liked kissing. After that he and I would meet in his basement for kissing lessons. Soon, of course, it came time for feeling lessons. He would feel my breasts and pubic area. I liked this exciting feeling, but I felt it was wrong somehow. The extent of my sex education was Mom saying, "Don't hold hands with boys or you'll have a baby." The only other thing she said was that boys never married a loose girl. "Don't let them touch you until you're married or else!" I was really scared, since I did a lot more than hold hands. Maybe that was where twins came from. My fear and guilt built up inside of me so badly that I skipped my period from nerves. When I told my Mom I hadn't gotten my "curse," she said flatly to me, "Did you fool around? Tell me the truth!" I confessed my sexual secrets—nights of French kisses, Mr. Handsome feeling up my tits and crotch. I was doomed. I noticed the relieved look on Mom's face, but she told me in her sternest voice, "Never do that again until you are married! And never tell your husband you did such filth or you'll lose him! Mark my words!"

After that, when my handsome boyfriend wanted to kiss me or be alone with me, I'd push him away and say, "Not until I'm married." Well, he never forced me, and we still watched "Batman" together. We still went for walks together, too, and I was under the impression that he was still my boyfriend.

One day all the kids were going swimming, and I went to his house to ask if he wanted to come with us. He was sitting in his backyard in a car that was up on cinder blocks. As I waved to him he beckoned me to come over. When I got close to the car I saw he was kissing and groping the naked tits of a fifteen-year-old girl. I stood there in shock. My face was red and warm and tears formed in my eyes. Not knowing what to say, I said, "You wanted me?" He meanly glared at me and said, "Get the boots on!" Then they both started laughing at me. I was shattered. I ran home blindly and sat in my backyard and cried my virginal teenage eyes out. We never spoke again. When I told Mom about it, she was proud of me. She said, "He might be with her, but he respects you." Big fucking deal!

Things have always turned around for me, though. Years later, when I was go-go dancing, I ran into my teenage heartthrob again. He was in his early thirties by then, still very handsome. He bought me a soda on my twenty-minute break, and we had a nice chat about old times. Then he took my hand, looked into my eyes, and said to me, "I'd love to get a relationship going. We could be great together. What do you say, babe?" I smiled back into his eyes and said in my sexiest Marilyn Monroe voice, "Get the boots on!"

I graduated from junior high in 1966. I was fourteen. No one came to my graduation. Then I went to Kennedy High for a while, but I quit when I was fifteen. Kennedy was the sister school of the famous East Side. No one was quite sure which was the roughest school. East Side was made famous in the 1988 movie, *Lean On Me*, the story of Principal Joe Clark, who tamed the school by carrying a baseball bat around. Well, the movie wasn't exaggerating. You needed a bat in those damn schools. I also quit because I wanted to work. The late 1960s were exciting for a teenager. I wanted to be in the world.

I knew a lot of guys who went to Vietnam. I wrote to sailor and soldier friends, pals in the Air Force and the Marines. One thing I noticed about all of them—they were all radically different when they came back. No one I knew who went to Vietnam did drugs before they left, but most of the ones who came back were card-carrying drug addicts with long hair. One guy I grew up with had wanted to be a state trooper so he could bust long-haired hippies who were polluting the air with pot. He went into the Air Force and was sent to Vietnam. By the time he got out, I didn't recognize him. He had hair down to his ass and was fucked up on drugs, the total opposite of what he had been. Another guy from North Fourth Street managed to survive Vietnam, but got killed his first night back. He and his drinking buddies were coming home from a drinking binge in New York, when they ran off the road, hit a fence, and flipped into a reservoir. Everybody in the car drowned.

I dated a lot of men who went to Vietnam and an equal number who claimed they had. I learned early on how to tell the ones who had really been there from the bullshit artists. The ones who went to Vietnam don't talk about it at all, or very little. They are not amused by shooting off fireworks on the Fourth of July. Often they don't sleep well. The bullshitters talk continually about "Nam." They start out, "No shit, but when I was in Nam . . ." In one of the go-go bars I worked in, a jerk was chopping my ear off about being a medic in Vietnam. He was trying his best to impress me by grossing me out with gruesome details. I didn't believe him, of course. No real vet talked like that. At one point, the fellow turned to the guy sitting next to him and said, "Buddy, you have no idea what it was like." In response the fellow took out his wallet and produced the laminated military I.D. card of a Vietnam medic.

By the time I was seventeen, I started going out with older, married men. By older, I mean men in their thirties. I had a problem, though. My virginity was getting in my way. I was losing one guy after another due to my Mom's creed, "Hold on to it no matter what!" Now, if you go out with a guy in his thirties, especially if he's married, he eventually wants to do more than hold hands. I put out some very sexual signals, but, really, I was not ready for this. Being that it was the late 1960s, I never wore anything more than a micro-miniskirt or dress, and low-cut blouses and tight sweaters. And I never wore (and still don't wear) any underpanties. I didn't (and don't) even own a pair. I was getting the reputation of being a "cock tease," but I never acted that way intentionally. It was just that my body wanted to do it, but my puritanical upbringing said not to.

I finally drove some poor bastard nuts, and I got what I was unintentionally signaling for. I went out with a nice guy who was thirty-three. I was almost eighteen. I wore a see-through blouse (no bra) and a black wool micro-miniskirt with, of course, no panties. To complete the ensemble, I had on black sheer pantyhose and silver platform high heels. I looked sensational, but I really didn't have a clue that I was teasing him. I let him kiss me and fondle me, and after I got him all worked up I said, "No." I was scared. I wasn't trying to be cute. The guy was a cop, so, of course, he had access to handcuffs. He said he wanted to show me how they worked. Now, looking back on this, I was either incredibly innocent or incredibly stupid, but I allowed myself to be handcuffed from behind. He started kissing me and grabbing me, and, before I knew it, he was painfully in me. He tore my pantyhose to shreds. This happened in the front seat of his car on a deserted lot. It was nighttime and cold. I remember looking up at the steam on the windows. Outside, I could see snow drifting down. It was over with fast. I thought sex lasted longer. He uncuffed my now-bleeding wrists and didn't say another word to me. I felt sore, embarrassed, and scared. I was bleeding and I didn't know why. Mom had never told me about this. It was too soon for my period, so why was I bleeding? Maybe my kidneys had popped. He drove in silence. He dropped me off at home and left without so much as a goodbye. Mom was awake. She noticed I was pale and visibly shaken. I thought she'd kill me, but I told her why I was trembling—and she reacted in a way I never expected. She was very gentle and understanding.

I never got another phone call from my date. From fear and guilt, I skipped two periods. Mom was convinced I was pregnant. I called up the cop to tell him, but he was very cool to me. "I can't be the father," he said. "How do I know I was the only one—you were no virgin, honey." I cried hysterically. "I was a virgin! There was blood!" Then he coolly said to me, "If there was blood, then bring me the clothing you wore, and I'll have it tested in the police lab. Until then, don't bother me. You're a whore and I can get seven guys who will swear they were with you. And by the way, your cunt was so damn tight it gave me blisters!" I was at a loss for words. All this time I was holding onto my sacred virginity, and when I finally lost it the event went totally unnoticed.

Mom kept my little secret from Pop. She knew he'd flip out. She managed to scrape up taxi fare so I could go to a doctor for a pregnancy test. Riding in the cold, drafty taxi, I felt scared and lost. I wanted to be a little girl again and have another chance. I was called into the doctor's office at once. He was a bald, bespeckled, short man with a cigarette dangling out of his mouth. After an embarrassing barrage of questions that seemed to go on forever, he asked me if I liked it. Sex. Then he told me it was "the only thing worth waking up for in the morning, like taking a shit." This pig then did a degrading examination of me with the stirrups, the bright fluorescent lights, the whole bit. He concluded that I was probably not with child, then gave me a needle to bring on my period. He said it should come within fourteen days. I asked, "Suppose it doesn't?"—to which he replied, "Then you're a mommy." Next!

Fourteen days later, no period! Mommy and I were both wrecks. I started crying hysterically. I asked Mom what would happen next. She said she would have to tell Pop that night, when he came home. Sick, I went back to bed and cried myself to sleep. I woke up about four o'clock in the afternoon. I was covered in blood! I was never so happy to see my period. I was giddy with relief. Mom and I hugged each other and danced around the kitchen. Our little secret was safe. Pop never found out, and Mommy and I were closer than ever.

Not too long after I lost my virginity I was brutally attacked again. And once again I blame no one but myself. Of course, I don't think it's O.K. to rape a girl, but it's also up to the girl not to put out the wrong signals. Like many teenage girls, I had a thing for fast cars, uniforms, and cute guys, usually the most rotten bastards I could hook up with. I wouldn't be caught dead with a nerd or a dork. I was a real cool breeze, or so I thought. In actuality, I was an accident looking for a place to happen. At some point I developed a new wrinkle—motorcycles and bikers. I got to meet quite a few of them hanging out in country and western bars.

It was mid-July, hotter than the devil's butt, and I was going to my girlfriend Inid's wedding. It was a country and western kind of wedding, meaning it was held in a crowded, sweltering apartment, spilling over into a redneck bar. I was wearing a long, paisley-print granny skirt (all the rage), a long-sleeved, black, ruffled, clinging see-through blouse, and black, patent-leather high heels. It was too hot for a wedding, but Inid was counting on me being there. She was a very nice girl, but majorly stupid. She let every guy she went out with take advantage of her, including her husband-to-be, Mike. I had known Mike before Inid met him. He was a bus driver who sometimes drove the bus I took home. He was handsome in a conceited sort of way and quite a ladies' man. Married, you ask? Of course. With three children. Mike tried to take me out when he met me, but I couldn't stand him, not because I didn't run around with married men, but because I hate conceited men. I took great delight in shooting him down. When Inid told me of her new heartthrob,

I did all that I could to discourage her. She wouldn't listen.

Mike's wife refused to give him a divorce (it was against her religion), so the son of a bitch poisoned her. One day I was with Inid getting a cold soda at the delicatessen next to the dress shop where we both worked. The soda can was so cold it had frost all over it. I was dying from thirst and this sight was very appealing to me. As I took a sip, my girlfriend dropped the bomb on me—she and her bus driver were going to get married, because he had poisoned his wife. I started to tremble all over. I spilled my soda all over my dress. A combination of thoughts raced through my mind. The biggest was for my girlfriend's safety. If that son of a bitch could kill one woman and get away with it, then he could kill her, too. The court found him not guilty because his wife technically died from a heart attack, and she had a history of a bad heart. On the other hand, my girlfriend had a reputation for exaggerating the truth, so maybe that story was just her overactive and very dramatic imagination.

Shortly after his wife's death, Mike popped the question to Inid. So, I found myself sweating my ass off in a church full of yahoos, knowing that the groom had murdered his wife to marry the dopey bride. The bridesmaids were wearing lovely blue gowns, but Inid was wearing a homemade, off-white gown with a stapled hemline. Maybe the dress wasn't short enough for her that morning, so she quickly stapled it up. I wouldn't put it past her. She was a real Okie.

After the wedding, it was back to the sweat-box apartment for food and alcohol. The reception was a total bust. The cold cuts weren't cold anymore. They had a sheen of sweat on them. The wedding cake was wilting. I could feel sweat trickling down between my breasts all the way to my stomach. I had nowhere to sit and I felt faint. Just before I was about to keel over, a nice bearded guy with tattoos asked me if I wanted to sit on his lap. Why not? I hit it off with the fellow right away. I'll call him Ron. It was time to go to the bar for more drinks and country western music! About eight cars of already loaded yahoos took off, with horns blaring that there'd just been a wedding—as if you couldn't grasp that fact by all the toilet-paper carnations and colored streamers decorating each beat-up hell wagon of a pickup truck. There I was, stuck in the middle, the only one who had the foresight to use deodorant. I'm not exaggerating. The bar was packed with people wearing cowboy hats and boots. A local country group filled the air with steel guitars. It sounded like heaven. Country western music sounds best live. I could listen to it all night. The singer had a voice like an angel. She sang sad love songs while her sequined costume picked up all the colored lights and threw them back out at the audience. I caught the bridal bouquet. It was lovely white tea roses, though pretty much wilted. Inid got drunk and passed out at the end of the bar, face down. Mike, who had been flirting with every girl in the place, started leering at me like a grinning ape. He pushed me against the wall and gave me a big, whiskey-laden kiss. I pushed him away, but he was much stronger than I was. Ron saw what was going on and came to my rescue. He offered to take me home. I liked being with Ron. I thought he was such a gentleman, coming to my defense and all.

Inid and Mike eventually got a divorce. He beat the hell out of her morning, noon, and night. He even forced her into prostitution so he didn't have to work. I haven't seen my girlfriend since 1978. She's gotten fat and now she drinks too much. She told me she was a go-go girl at one point and planned to remarry. She asked me to attend the wedding, but I let it go. I had to move on. She depressed me, and we really had nothing in common.

I started to see much of Ron. We were together every night. He never really took me out to any nice places, only from one bar to another. I wasn't too keen on this because, for one, I didn't drink, and, two, I had had enough bar hopping when I was a kid. I noticed Ron drank quite a bit, but you couldn't mention it to him because he would get very defensive. I did once and he told me I was just a kid, what did I know? I was nineteen; he was thirty-eight. Ron was a motorcycle enthusiast, an owner of three Harley-Davidsons. His friends were a little unnerving. They were all bar people and bikers, the real thing, bearded, tattooed, and sweaty. Ron and his friends always wore jeans and t-shirts. Ron added a bandana around his head that made him look like some kind of Indian. He had been married, but got divorced. He had daughters close to my age.

Ron told me that if I slept with him he would take me for a ride on his bike, but not until then. After my experience with the cop and the pregnancy scare, I slept with no one, despite all my worldliness. I was scared out of my wits, so I always had some excuse not to have sex. Still, I continued to dress very seductively. I was a frightened child in a slut's body. I shudder when I think of how cheap I used to look. But I wanted to ride on the back of a Harley very badly. Ron knew this and held it over my head. After I'd make out passionately with the poor bastard, making him crazy, I'd say, "No! Stop! I can't!" I didn't realize that if I had no intention of going all the way, then I shouldn't have let it go past a friendly kiss. But I was very passionate and liked making out wildly.

We would fight all the time over the same thing—sex. One day Ron told me he was taking me on a picnic in upper New York State on the back of his bike. I was thrilled. Pop wasn't home and my mother was mad as hell at the way I left the house—white hot-pants, an orange see-through blouse (no bra, as usual), and white sandals. I very confidently hopped on the back of the bike, immediately burning my leg on the exhaust pipe. We were off to the woods for a picnic. A picnic with no basket? I was scared shitless on the back of the bike, my leg hurt like hell, but I was too cool to admit it. I was leaning the wrong way and almost caused the bike to dump. I was pissing Ron off. Twice Ron had to pull over and tell me how to lean. I felt like a chastised child. We came to a cabin off the main road. There were dogs tied up in the yard and the smell of dog shit everywhere. Motorcycles, together and in pieces, were strewn all about the yard, and beer cans were piled high in garbage cans. The place smelled worse inside. There was a filthy mattress on the floor, dirty clothes scattered about, and beer cans crushed alongside the mattress. Stretched out on the mattress was a dirty-looking guy with an unshaven face, messy hair, and long, yellow toenails. He smelled like an unwashed crotch. I was totally grossed out. Then Ron told me the guy was his best friend.

The more I saw, the more I wanted to be back home. The great bike ride was no great shakes, and the guy I was dating was a bum. We had to wait for the rest of the jolly picnickers to meet us at the cabin. I was told to make myself comfortable. That was a laugh. Where the hell could I sit? Within the hour, an army of bikes thundered in. Ron told me never to call them motorcycles. Only fags said motorcycle. The new arrivals had two pickup trucks behind them. On the backs of the Harleys were female versions of the scrungy guy I'd just met. Sure enough, they had the picnic supplies—beer by the case, Jack Daniels whiskey by the truckload. I couldn't help but wonder what liquor store they had knocked over. Then came the drugs. Now I was really scared. All these people were in their thirties, and here I was, all of nineteen and stupid. The guys looked at me as if I had no clothes on, which I practically didn't. The women looked at me the same way! I wanted to put on lead-lined underwear.

In no time flat we were on our merry way. My heart was in my mouth. We rode off into the woods and came upon a clearing. It was nice, with lots of trees and a small hill with a pond on the other side of it. The festivities began. Drugs and booze were in full swing. The women took off their tops to expose sagging, stretch-marked breasts and started cooking the sacrificial beast for dinner over a barbeque grill. I saw Ron using drugs and drinking his ass off just like the others. I knew he drank, but I didn't know he fucked around with drugs, and there I was sipping a can of cherry soda. Some wiseass biker came up to me and said, "Drink all the cherry soda you want, but it'll never grow back." He gave me the creeps. Then the bikers started driving their bikes (dirt bikes) down the grassy hill and jumping into the pond.

After dinner they started an orgy on blankets spread all over the place. Ron came up to me and started getting romantic. I pushed him away. He sickened me and I demanded he take me home. Ron got pissed off and stormed away. I heard him talking to a big furry biker who had been eye-balling me all day. The big biker laughed, then strolled over to me with his potbelly hanging over his half-zipped jeans. "Hey, little girl, I hear you ain't about to put out. Is that true? Well see, if you don't give us a little poontang, then you walk home, O.K." I was mad now and yelled in his face, "Fine!" Then I headed through the woods for the highway, confident I could hitch a ride home. I wasn't getting off that easy. Now all eyes were upon me. The big burly guy followed me and dragged me back by my long red hair. I was kicking and screaming obscenities at him, but he only laughed. Then he smacked me in the mouth so hard I hit the ground. I tasted something salty. It was my own blood, dripping from my mouth into the dirt. Next, he and I were encircled by bikes with their headlights turned on. The big guy stood me up, dusted me off, and said, "Are you O.K., sis?" Then with one hand he tore my blouse off, the little orange buttons scattering all over. I started acting strangely. I fell to my knees and started looking for my buttons. I kept saying, "Where's my other button?" I was crawling around the ground, feeling the dirt for my buttons. I found one and it was as though I'd found the Hope Diamond. I looked at it and held it tightly. The next thing I knew, the big biker was sliding my hot-pants off and lying on top of me. There were about nine bikers in all. I just stared straight up at the sky and watched it turn dark. I squeezed the button in my hand like it was some kind of tran-quility stone and put my mind out of my body to a place that was beautiful. When they were done with me, I remember lying there in the dirt covered with blood and sperm. They poured beer on me at one point and it dried up in my hair. It wasn't long before the biker women had their sport with me. They picked me up and dragged me down the grassy hill to the pond. There they punched me in the stomach, knocking the wind out of me, then held my head under water until I thought my lungs would explode. Ron never participated. I saw him standing by a tree with tears running down his face.

Eventually I was lying in the back seat of a car that belonged to one of the biker chicks. I was cold even though someone had thrown in a blanket for me. Ron came and sat next to me. He brushed my hair out of my face and said, "I'm so sorry. Just for the record, I didn't get involved." I just said in a hoarse whisper, "Take me home." I was taken back to the filthy little cabin and cleaned up by the biker chicks. Then I was given a dirty pair of jeans to wear that were too big, and a red plaid lumberjack shirt. I think Ron felt bad because he thought of his own daughter, who was seventeen, two years younger than I was. Who knows. I found out he was also an ex-con.

It was late by the time they took me home. Mom was asleep and Pop was out on the truck. My brother was out with his own friends. I went into the bathroom and ran the water. A couple of cockroaches ran for their lives. I looked in the mirror. Under the bat-winged light, I saw a puffy face with swollen lips. After I soaked in a hot tub for what seems like hours, Mom came in to take a pee. She took one look at me and shook her head sadly. Then she asked me what time I got in. She told me I looked like hell and that I had better stop the late nights or I would ruin my looks. She was right. I never told her or anybody what happened to me, because I was so ashamed and embarrassed by my wiseass behavior.

A month passed and I was relieved of my fear of being impregnated by one of those Neanderthals. I was very lucky. All I got was an infection that wasn't serious. I never saw Ron again, no love lost, and I stayed home at night more often. I was a changed person. I withdrew into myself and rarely conversed with anyone. I preferred the company of animals and my records. Mom noticed the difference in me, but she was just grateful that I was home at night. She never asked questions. I began to respect my mother for being much wiser than I.

I never climbed on the back of a bike again until I posed for the cover of *Iron Horse* magazine, a bikers girlie magazine. I did it to put an old fear to rest, and I succeeded. The editor asked me if I had ever had any experiences with "motorcycles." I could tell he certainly hadn't, because only fags say "motorcycle." To this day I wince when I hear the sound of bikes rumbling.

I once went out with a politician. He was crazy about me. He was not married (something new to me at the time), but he didn't want to be seen with me. He said it would hurt his chances in an upcoming election. Still, he couldn't see enough of me on the sly. He particularly loved my black leather miniskirt and thigh-high leather boots. He even told me that he loved me once, but that marriage would be out of the question. Then he had the brass balls to say, "I'll be marrying soon. A good politician has to marry a proper wife. But can we still see each other?" I told him to take a flying fuck and left.

A few months down the road, his wedding was reported in the papers. His wife was as plain as a bowl of oatmeal. There stood my old boyfriend, prim and proper, a beacon to society with his proud and faithful woman by his side. I wondered if he secretly made her wear leather boots and walk all over him like I had to. He continued to call me after his marriage, but I dusted him.

We moved to a better neighborhood, and I started working in a dress shop downtown. It was 1972 and one of my North Fourth Street neighbors was arrested for beating his wife and three small children to death with a hammer. They were all friends of mine. I was in shock. I heard he left a note explaining why he did it. He said he was having a homosexual affair at work, and his lover was blackmailing him with threats to tell his wife. So, in order to save his wife and kids the humiliation, he killed them. This information came from a member of the ambulance crew. They were the first ones on the scene. We all thought he was gay but that he was O.K., just a little feminine. I understand he will be getting out of jail soon.

In the winter of 1971 a terrible accident helped save my parents' lives. They had been drinking heavily practically since the day they met, almost twenty years. One day I arranged with Mom to meet her at the bus stop when I came home from work so I could walk her to the liquor store. Supplies to get tanked for the week had to be laid in. Well, I got off work, caught the bus, came to my stop, and got off. It was snowing, and down the road I could see Mom laboring to reach me. As I got closer to her I could see she was tipsy. She was weaving from side to side. Suddenly—and I did see it coming—Mom fell. I rushed up to her, and she was lying on the ground groaning. Sure enough, she broke her leg.

Well, I got her to the hospital and Pop came, all shaken. Mom and Pop looked at each other, and right then and there they decided to go on the wagon. And they did. God does work in mysterious ways.

Every day I would get the bus on the street corner where I lived. Being nineteen years old, I knew it all, or so I thought. One hot sunny day, while waiting for my bus, I saw a young man getting coffee from a luncheonette across the street. When he saw me in my miniskirt, high heels, and long, flame-red hair, he meandered across the street to investigate. The guy was very tall, slim, and quite handsome. His hair was brown with sun streaks in it. His eyes were what struck me most. They were pale blue and could stare right through you. He was wearing a bright red shirt and black chinos.

He said, "Did anyone ever tell you that you're beautiful?" What corn! That had to be the oldest line in captivity, but I fell for it. He said the bus wasn't coming on time. It had broken down—maybe I should let him give me a ride. Transfixed by his eyes, I said, "What makes you such an expert on the buses?" He replied, "I'm a bus driver." Well, I didn't have an answer to that. He looked married. I can tell a married man a million miles away. By that time in my life I didn't want to get involved with a married man, and I told him so. "I don't care how blue your eyes are." He replied that he used to be married, but now he was divorced. I'd heard that chestnut before, so I asked him if I looked like I had just stepped off a hay wagon with a duck tucked under my arm. All married men use that ploy. He asked me out to dinner. I told him no. I knew he was married, and I wouldn't date him for that reason, plus he was lying to me. Exasperated, he said, "What do I have to do to prove I'm divorced, show you my divorce papers?" I said that would do. "When I see your divorce papers, I'll go out with you." I was sure this would get rid of him. No. The next day he met me at the corner while I waited for my bus. He had a smug twinkle in his eyes as he presented me with divorce papers, notarized and all. I felt like a nickel waiting for change.

I had dinner with him that night, and I had dinner with him every night for the next seven years. Before I knew it, I was married to the young man with the blue eyes, Jim Lambert. Our marriage was turbulent, to say the least. We were both too young and pig-headed. Worst of all, we were both Pisces. Anyone who's into astrology can tell you that two people of the same sign shouldn't marry. After seven years of fireworks, we got divorced, but not before one wonderful thing came out of it—our son Jack, who was born in 1974. Jim and I are good friends now. He specializes in outdoor photography, and he is one of my trusted photographers. As long as we don't live with each other we'll be fine. Two lager heads don't mix.

When I married Jim, at the age of nineteen, I became an instant mother. After his first divorce, Jim found himself the single parent of his cute little boy, Jimmy. The boy was not quite three years old when I first met him. He had flame-red hair and huge blue eyes. I wanted to love him and be close to him, but he didn't want me. He cried for his natural mom almost every night. He resented me. My heart went out to the little fellow. Jimmy's mother was a teenage girl like me, scared and mixed up. She rarely came to see him. In time Jimmy and I became very close. I loved him like my own child and he loved me. I raised him until he was ten years old, and then I had to let him go, due to complications in my divorce from Jim. Jimmy went to live with his grandparents. This broke my heart. I never stopped loving him and I never will. He was my first son. I was there when he was scared or when he got sick on mangos and Yoo-hoo. That little boy is a grown man now. He's nineteen, six-foot-three, and in the Air Force.

When I left Jim I moved in with my Mom and Dad. I had shabby clothes, no boots for the winter, no money, and, above all, no self-esteem or self-respect. I didn't know how to talk to people anymore. I put on weight and my nose was crooked.

One day, after walking my son to school in the snow, I passed a television repair shop. A very smart-looking, well-dressed man came out and started talking to me. He asked me where my boots were.

I was wearing shoes with open backs, no socks or pantyhose, and no gloves. I was trembling in the cold. I told him I had no money for them.

Well, every day after that Carmen met me and we would talk. Finally he asked me out. I was scared. I hadn't dated in seven years. I didn't remember how to dress or act. But I agreed, as long as we went to a place where I wouldn't have to dress fancy.

He took me to a seafood restaurant in New York's Greenwich Village. Afterwards he took me to a fine shoe store and bought me a very expensive pair of boots. Then he took me to a clothing store and bought me some warm clothes and a coat. He asked for nothing in return. Carmen helped me get a good lawyer so I could get a divorce. I started seeing a lot of Carmen. He was very good for my self-esteem. He helped me to overcome my depression and feel better about myself. He was always there for me, no matter what. Whenever I felt down, I could call up Carmen, even if it was 1:00 A.M. and he was sleeping. He'd listen to my high anxiety and then tell me to give him ten minutes. He'd get dressed, come and pick me up, and take me to the Village for cannolis and cappuccino. He'd build me up and tell me he had a feeling I'd be famous some day.

I felt good hearing this, but I didn't believe in myself like he did. But thanks to Carmen I started treating myself a little better. I got a good job as a restaurant hostess, I had a beautiful wardrobe, I lost weight, and I started living in peace with my parents and small son.

Sometime after I left Jim, I got a job as a barmaid in a bar patronized almost exclusively by Yugoslavians and Albanians. Now, me being a hot-tempered Irish girl, I was in no mood to take much shit from these people. The story starts when I got a job as a hostess in a little restaurant owned by a Yugoslavian woman named Nell. This character was slippery—she was wanted by the police, the IRS, the FBI, and the immigration service. She "just slipped out the back, Jack," whenever anyone came looking for her. Nell also owned a bar on the other side of town. One day, while I was handling the lunchtime crowd, Nell suddenly told me I was going to work as a barmaid at her bar—that night. I told slippery Nell that I knew nothing about serving or mixing drinks. She told me that was O.K., she would teach me. She promised me good pay.

Nell drove me to the bar. It was a very lovely lounge and banquet hall. It had a long bar with a load of thirsty Yugoslavian and Albanian men draped over it. This was the extent of my training: Nell opened the bar gate, shoved me in, and said, "I'll see you." Well, after some trial and error, I worked out a routine. The customers told me how to mix drinks, and I caught on fast. Still, every night I'd come home smelling like a bar rag from all the liquor I had spilled.

For the first week, all went well, although there were signs something was wrong. For one thing, the men were basically crazy. They were always looking for a fight. Most of them carried guns and knives. One night I walked in to see a guy cleaning his gun on the bar. I felt like I was in some foreign country. The jukebox had nothing but Yugoslavian and Albanian songs, which I did not understand or like. As the days went by, the men started making dirty remarks to me and insinuating that American women were sluts. They'd drink straight cognac and then throw the glass at the cash register. The first night I cleaned up the broken glass from about twenty shot glasses. The next night I just left it there, so all night I walked over crunchy glass.

One guy sat at the bar drinking down one shot of cognac after another. When he was done, he went berserk and stuck a fork in his own head and had to be rushed to the hospital.

Another character called himself James Bond. He first introduced himself to me by pulling a switchblade and sticking it under my chin. This scared the hell out of me and I was willing to quit then and there, but he was only kidding. After that it became a joke with us. He'd come in and pull the switchblade on me and I would say, "How you doing tonight, Bond?" One night he came in and forgot to pull the knife on me. To show you how crazy I was getting, I felt hurt that he forgot.

The bar had rooms upstairs, and it was common knowledge that the cocktail waitresses were going upstairs with the customers to go "Rolling for Dollars." Nell was a pimp and so was her partner, Russ, a short, conceited man who wore pretentious diamond pinky rings and gold stickpins. He always draped his coat over his shoulders like a cape and strutted around the lounge acting like King Shit. He would hold out his hand, and all the cocktail waitresses would kiss it. He made the mistake of extending his hand to me once in front of a crowded bar. I was very busy and very rushed. He said, "Kiss my hand." I glared back at him and said, "I'll kiss your hand when you kiss my ass!" The bar went wild with laughter and he lost face. A little while later, while I was cracking ice, Russ came up to me and said, "Go upstairs. A man just paid me plenty of money for you." I said, "Not me Jack, I'm just a barmaid. If he paid you plenty then *you* go upstairs and bend over!"

In all fairness, I did meet some very nice men there, too. One guy was an Albanian about twenty years old. He offered to take me home after work. I went with him, since he was a gentleman. He asked me if he could buy me something to eat at a diner. I was hungry, so we went for a bite to eat. I ordered a BLT and he ordered plain cheesecake. I offered him a piece of my sandwich when I saw he didn't know what a BLT was, but when he saw it had bacon on it he nearly went wild—eating bacon was against his religion or something. After turning down a nice BLT, he then smothered his cheesecake in ketchup! Now it was my turn to go wild!

One night that week an ex-con just released from prison came to the bar. It was his old watering hole. He was a celebrity there. All the customers looked up to him. They bought him drinks all night long. Now, this guy was very nice to me. He was Albanian, looked like Peter Cushing, and was quiet. He tipped me well and treated me with the utmost respect. I liked him. That night some wiseass decided to pour booze into the jukebox and shorted it out. Now there was no music. The go-go girls, arriving to dance on two chairs and a plank, took one look and left. I was told to jump up on the plank and dance to these assholes clapping their hands. "Not me!" This made them mad, so they grabbed a new cocktail waitress and start pawing her tits and grabbing her pubic area. She was young and scared and started crying. I got a pool stick and went after the bastards. I gave her cab fare and sent her home. Now I was really on their shit list. But I was hot, too. Finally, some jerk came up to me and said, in his language, "your mother's cunt." I took the hose from behind the bar and squirted him down with club soda. Now talk was buzzing around the bar in Yugoslavian and Albanian. They were pointing to me as they spoke. Then King Shit came out and said to me, "Apologize to my friend for wetting him." I said, "his mother's cunt" in Yugoslavian. Russ grabbed my wrist. I took a filthy bar rag and threw it in his face. Russ stormed away.

Now, the ex-con friend of mine was sitting quietly during this entire donnybrook. He said to me, "Let me take you home tonight." Because he was so nice and I was too upset to wait for a taxi, I agreed. No one stood in our way when we left. All seemed to be frightened of him. He told me the reason he was so insistent that I go home with him was that the men around the bar were saying they were going to teach the American bitch a lesson. "They were planning to cut your tongue out in the alley next to the lounge. But they know better than to start with me. I saved your life." I thanked him. We went to breakfast and he said, "I would like to make you my wife." Then he said, "I must tell you, though, I'm a very jealous man. If I ever see you so much as talk to another man, I will cut your heart out." I asked him what he had been in prison for. He said he had raped his wife with a knife then cut her heart out because she was talking to another man. When he dropped me off that night, I quit that job and didn't go back for my pay.

I met David in 1978, when I was working a part-time job as a hostess in a Greek restaurant. My job was to look good, make reservations, make sure no one seated themselves, and see that the waitresses had equal numbers of tables. After a hectic day of waitresses bitching at me, ladies bringing strollers into the restaurant when they weren't allowed to, and old Greeks pinching me on the can, I was in a foul mood. In walked a tall, very handsome young businessman. He strutted right past me. Well, I wasn't about to have that. That's what I was there for, to seat the customers, and he wasn't going to seat himself even if I had to wrestle him to the ground. I was getting tired of this ignore-the-hostess bit. I grabbed a menu and followed him, calling out, "Table for one, sir?" David looked down at me and smiled, "No, thank you. I'm going to the bar." I had no jurisdiction over the bar, so I had to let him go.

However, I started making excuses to walk past him in the bar. I wanted him to notice me, and I wanted to see if he had a wedding band on. He was checking me out, too. He later said he was looking at me from the corners of his eyes. In fact, he was straining his eyes so hard that the bartender, who was on the other side of him, saw him looking straight ahead, but with only the whites of his eyes showing. David told me goodbye as he left, but he said he'd be back. He was.

When I fell in love with David, I was still legally married to my first husband. We were separated and I was with David, and Jim was with someone, too. David and I wanted to marry but it would be at least two years before I could afford a divorce. In the meantime, I was diagnosed as having a benign, "fibroid" tumor on my cervix. The doctor told me I needed a hysterectomy. Of course, this would rule out children for David. I had Jack from my first marriage, but David had never been married. He said it didn't matter—he just wanted me, and, as far as he was concerned, Jack was like his own son. I wouldn't hear of it. I told David if I couldn't give him a child then I would not marry him.

I went to two other doctors for their opinions. Both said that a hysterectomy was not necessary, but that pregnancy was not likely. One doctor told me, "You can try, but you'll probably miscarry at three months." That night at dinner I decided I'd try to give David a child. I told David if we wanted a baby it had to be now. So, we agreed to get me pregnant despite the fact that I was still legally married, despite what our parents would say, and despite the whole damn puritanical attitude. Screw convention!

After many blissful tries I became pregnant. We were beside ourselves with joy. When David gave his parents the news, they accused me of stupidity for getting myself "knocked-up." When we tried to explain that we had planned it, they didn't believe us. David's mother offered me money for an abortion.

David and I moved in together. I got my divorce by the skin of my teeth, looking like a small watermelon in court. Thank goodness it was winter and I was covered in a big coat. We were now free to marry. We did not. I wanted to wait until the baby was born to see how David was with babies—plus, I refused to have wedding photos taken while I was pregnant. In years to come, our child might think he or she forced us to get married. Our parents thought we were nuts. Our baby would be a love child, a bastard! Who gives a shit!

The baby came, a nine-pound, eleven-ounce baby girl, Juliet March. David was wonderful with the baby and never once did he slight Jack. So, on December 1, 1979, two months after Juliet was born, David and I were wed. And, for good measure, Juliet's birth corrected my tumor. I didn't need an operation, and I can still have kids if I want to.

The year after Juliet was born, I felt an itch. I wanted to do something outside the house. At this same time I was wondering—did I still have my figure? Did David *really* see a gorgeous woman when he came home at night?

One day I had a bright idea. I thought maybe it would be fun to see if I could successfully pull off a strip act. Why not? I was good-looking enough! That night I brought up the idea to David. He was skeptical, but not opposed, exactly. Now, one thing about David is that he is not a "macho man." He does not put his foot down to me. This does not make him a wimp. He just believes in women's right to make up their own minds. He is not like many men, who feel emasculated if their wives work. As far as other men looking at me, well, David is secure. He is proud of me and very supportive. He agreed I should strip if I really wanted to.

The Minx

We went to New York City to look around. We passed by a number of burlesque theaters. One had "Girls Wanted" signs in the window. I knew what stripping was, but I had never seen it performed. David took me into the Follies Burlesque theater. We walked up a long, narrow stairway that smelled like a combination of urine and perfume. At the top of the stairs we were stopped by a huge young man and an old man. They told us the show contained nudity. They wanted to make sure that, as a woman, I would not be offended. I assured them I wouldn't and pushed past them. This was a new and frightening experience for me. The theater was dark, the stage lit up in red. Men sat quietly waiting for the show to start. David and I took our seats. I took in every aspect of the theater. Girls in bathrobes swished past us on their way out to the lobby. I was the only woman in the audience, so I got a lot of curious looks from the strippers.

The announcer came on stage. He introduced a dancer and the music began. Out from between red velvet curtains stepped a lovely oriental woman. She was a terrific dancer. She twirled around and around in a cloud of shimmering chiffon. I sat through several other dancers and soon I was sold. I wanted to become a stripper.

It wasn't the first time in my life I'd entertained the thought of becoming a stripper. As a child, perhaps about seven years old, I had seen *Gypsy,* a movie starring Natalie Wood. Right there and then I wanted to be a stripper. I told Mom I wanted to become a burlesque queen, "just like Gypsy." When the smoke cleared, I couldn't sit down for a month. I remember practicing little strip acts in front of my mom's bedroom mirror. I used her size-nine high heels. My grandmother's woolen shawl was my mink stole. I tried to obscure its sweaty smell by squirting it down with Mom's favorite perfume.

By the time I was about nine, I was giving little strip shows in my girlfriend's basement. All the little boys in the neighborhood would come. For a dime I'd pull down my Mickey Mouse reflecto panties. For a quarter, the boys could put a Band-Aid on my butt. Mom never found out. "Straws in the wind."

My mother used to love to shock the neighbors by saying she had been a stripper in her youth. After a suitable pause, she would then tell them that she had worked in a plastic factory called "Color-forms." She was employed to strip plastic from between Popeye's legs with her fingernail, hence, on her official worksheet, they put her down as "stripper."

After sitting through the seven dancers at the burlesque theater, I went out to the manager to ask for a job. The boss was an old man who walked with a limp. He hired me immediately, without even seeing my act—not that I had one. It was winter, and I was wearing a thick fur coat and mucklucks. He didn't even know how my figure was. Nevertheless, I was to show up on Monday. This left me the whole weekend to put an act together.

I didn't know the first thing about putting a strip act together. I knew I had to be on stage twenty minutes. I asked a stripper who was getting a soda in the lobby what I should do for music. She told me to pick out five or six songs, time them to arrange a twenty-minute set, then get them taped professionally. She told me where to go to get them taped.

I spent all night going over my record collection, which, I may add, was and is extensive. I chose a set of songs I knew I could dance to easily, remembering to put one slow and sexy song toward the end of the tape. This was for floor work, expected of all the strippers. One song I was very proud to dance to was "Shangrila." I thought it was so sexy. Next, I put together a strip costume. I emulated the strippers I'd seen on stage the night before. They wore mainly G-strings with long shirts thrown over them and high heels. My costume was a go-go costume of red sequins, a skimpy G-string, and an equally skimpy bra. I threw one of David's long, button-down black shirts over it, and I wore black strapless pumps with four-inch heels. I put a kelly-green scarf of chiffon around my neck. My hair dresser had given it to me for good luck. With my hair in a long, straight, platinum-blonde Cleopatra and my eyes painted like a cat, I was ready for burlesque. But was burlesque ready for me?

Monday arrived. I was on edge as David and I approached the theater. Suddenly I noticed—my name on the marquee! It read, "The Minx." I was instantly flushed with pride. I had never seen my "name" in lights before. It felt good.

We went up those narrow, urine-smelling stairs. An old stripper was taking tickets. She actually tried to make me pay to get into the theater! David pushed past her, going through the turnstile. It clicked two customers on the meter, but there would be no money to account for us at the end of the night, when they tallied up the take. This caused a commotion, as if I wasn't nervous enough. The old stripper had a heck of a filthy mouth, but I had other things on my mind. The boss was thrilled to see me show up early. It's a habit I've always had. I met the bouncer, a young man about six-foot-six, two hundred and fifty pounds. Later I found out he liked children, specifically little girls, and not in a fatherly way.

I was ushered backstage to meet the other strippers. The dressing rooms were little cubicles with mirrors and makeup tables. There were nails driven into the walls to hang up your costumes. The cubicles had doors, but nobody kept them closed, except the star stripper. She refused to mingle with the low-life, fill-in strippers, commonly known as silver-star dancers. The boss told me I would share a dressing room with one of the girls. He didn't tell *her,* however, and she wasn't about to share her crowded cubicle with me. When the boss left us alone to get acquainted, she told me to get out and that if I went back and told the boss the strippers would knock the hell out of me. These were girls to think twice about. There was a black, six-foot-tall whip bitch, all decked out in black leather, carrying a huge cat-o'-nine-tails with razor blades attached to the ends. She took an immediate hatred to me. There was a girl with a dirty mouth, covered in tattoos. There was a lesbian stripper with two long, sagging breasts and large, owl-eye glasses. They called her the "Angel," and she was pregnant. She went out of her way to be tough and hard. There was the old stripper who took tickets. She was still pissed off about the turnstile. There was also another old stripper, who kept her distance, and the oriental girl, who was civil to me but preoccupied with using makeup to cover large black bruises on her body, gifts from her boyfriend. Finally, there was the "Star." She was about six feet tall and quite pretty. She wore a silly-ass feather-head piece that made her even taller. She told everyone she had been a Las Vegas show girl. When she walked out on stage, she swept the ceiling. She liked to hole up in her "star" dressing room, with its large gold star on the door.

My first time stripping I made enemies with the Star. By coincidence I had chosen the same song for my floor work as she used —"Shangrila." The Star was furious when she found out. She brought the boss backstage and confronted me. She demanded I scrap the "Shangrila" number because she was the star, while I was just a lowly, half-assed, fill-in stripper who wasn't going to amount to anything. She punctuated her tirade by stamping her size-ten foot in temper. I looked her square in the eye and said no, and the boss didn't insist on it.

This increased my isolation among the strippers, but I couldn't have cared less. I was losing heart. Stripping seemed like a mistake. The girls were making life miserable for me. They made me dress in the hall, and it was cold there. I had to hang my clothes on doorknobs. They wouldn't even let me look in their mirrors, so I had to bring my own to do my makeup and to change in front of. Finally it was time to go on. I felt sick. The girls were snickering and making mean remarks. I stood behind the red velvet curtain, waiting for my introduction. My heart was beating so hard and fast it sounded like it was in my head. My palms were sweating, and my face got a nervous twitch on one side. Finally, I heard the announcer introduce me as a newcomer to the theater. "Let's have a big hand for the Mink." The Mink! He'd mispronounced my name. I was off to a good start. I had difficulty making my way through the folds of the curtains. I got a round of applause and a little giggling, but mostly encouraging faces. David was in the front row for support. The strippers were sitting in the front row, too, laughing and putting their feet up on the stage. One of them started to strip, distracting the audience from watching me. The Angel yelled up, "The Minx stinks!" I was so nervous I forgot to do my floor work. The floor was so slippery I thought for sure I would slip. I kept my eye on David, who was cheering me on. I felt better knowing he was there. Soon I'd finished. It had gone faster than I'd expected. The audience gave me a large round of applause. I'd done it.

Curiously, when I went backstage, the other strippers came up to congratulate me and compliment my act. Even the Angel said she was sorry, not to pay any attention to what she'd said. Finally, one of the girls took all my stuff out of the hallway and put it into her room. I had been accepted.

Working in burlesque requires long hours, but easy ones. My shows were only twenty minutes, and then I was off for two, sometimes three hours, free to do as I pleased. I could see a movie, go to sleep, or do anything. Mainly, I chose to sit in the audience and study the other strippers' moves, then try to improve upon them. At first the other dancers thought I was a lesbian, but I soon set them right.

In between acts the theater played music while the next stripper got ready to go on. This enabled the patrons to stretch their legs, go to the bathroom, or check the race papers. Our Neanderthal bouncer was very fond of one particular song, Johnny Paycheck's "Take This Job and Shove It." He was in charge of the music, so he blasted this country western delight over the sound system every chance he got. He never deviated from that one song. I think he was trying to tell the management something. The song was not exactly a crowd-pleaser, and it was no mood-setter either. Patrons and strippers, he was driving us all crazy.

As the performances went by, I gained more and more confidence in myself and my act. I had started developing technique, but I didn't have a gimmick. I noticed both good dancers and bad dancers had gimmicks, like the Star's feather headdress and Vegas routine. I was blasé, no more than a glorified go-go girl. As the weeks passed, I noticed how much better the star strippers were treated. I asked the boss how to go about being a star dancer. He took a look at me and said, "The star dancers were either porno queens or show girls, or they've been dancing a long time. You don't have the experience or a gimmick. Be happy we let you dance. Never mind being a star."

Naturally, my determination to improve my act only increased. I started searching for my gimmick. I noticed that none of the girls were doing an actual striptease. They whipped their clothes off in five minutes, then rolled around on the floor for lack of anything else to do. Their music was often loud rock with a very fast pace. Not all the patrons, particularly the older men, cared for the heavy rock beat. During my break, I would sit in the lobby and ask the men what they liked and what they expected to see, or wanted to see, in a burlesque show. The answers were interesting. First of all, the older men told me that this was not burlesque at all. It was nice and sexy, but not burlesque. They told me that old-time burlesque was a variety show, and the girls had more pride in their acts. Burlesque back then was a whole comedy show. In addition to strippers, there were baggy-pants comedians, or "top bananas," comedy teams, and plenty of show girls. Burlesque does not mean "strip show." It means variety, comedy, song, and dance. At first burlesque didn't have strippers. Later on, to punch up the old, stale jokes, strippers were added, making burlesque what it is known as today. A lot of people say that strippers ruined burlesque, but after hearing countless old burlesque jokes with "what the hey" as the punch line, I believe burlesque would have died like vaudeville if it had not been for strippers.

Looking for my gimmick, I studied old-time burlesque with a vengeance. I read books by Minsky, the biggest name in burlesque. I read books by famous queens of burlesque like Gypsy Rose Lee and the great Ann Corio, who was only sixteen when she got into burlesque. I saw plays about old-time burlesque and interviewed people who had performed in old-time burlesque shows. I really did my homework. I had my gimmick.

Stripping was definitely not burlesque anymore. There were no comedy routines, although some strip acts I saw could have qualified. Strippers didn't dance to sexy music anymore, and bumps and grinds were obsolete. There weren't too many long gowns anymore, and the tantalizing art of taking off one glove at a time was a thing of the past. I decided to try my hand at an old-world burlesque act, complete with long gown, opera gloves, and pearls. I wore long, elegant rhinestone earrings and diamond clips in my hair. I wrapped myself in a feather boa and used sexy perfume. I put together a slow, sexy strip tape, with no rock music. I combed the record stores for saxophone music and heavy drumbeat music, anything that fit a certain sexy sound I was looking for. Once I had put everything together, I was a little scared. A Times Square audience shows no mercy. What if I came off as corny? It was a chance I was going to have to take.

On the day of my big debut, the hall was packed. We had a lot of dignified men in that day. Contrary to popular belief, the Times Square audience is not necessarily just a bunch of sleazeballs. We had judges, lawyers, people from Wall Street, even doctors. Don't get me wrong—the sleazeballs were mixed in, but what would Times Square be without sleazeballs?

As I dressed, I felt my heart pounding wildly, just like my first time stripping. The other strippers were quiet as I walked past them to the curtain. Suddenly, the announcer introduced me. "Today we proudly introduce the Minx, doing old-time burlesque." I heard my music start. The drums were loud and stimulating. I closed my eyes for a second before I went out on stage. I felt transformed. I felt back in time. To me, this was real burlesque.

By the time I got out on stage I wasn't nervous anymore. I felt very much in control. My colleagues lined up against the wall to watch me. Even the ticket takers ran in to watch when they heard the bump and grind music. The audience was rapt. I acted like a queen of burlesque. When I finished, the whole place applauded wildly. The other dancers whistled and clapped excitedly. This was the first time I ever saw, much less received, a standing ovation. It would not be the last. I was now a gold star dancer. I had my gimmick.

I had also proven myself. That was all I really wanted to do when I started on this stripping lark. I saw no real reason to continue, so in a few weeks I quit. I'd be back, however, after an odyssey I could never have predicted at the time.

My mother died that year, in 1981. It was the week after her sixtieth birthday. She started complaining to me that it hurt to sit down. She also had some bleeding. I noticed that she had hardly any appetite at all and seemed to be losing weight—a once large, robust woman. I made an appointment with a doctor, which she thought ludicrous. My parents never went to doctors. They used to diagnose themselves, a practice that enraged me. I had to go to the doctor with her because she was so scared and childlike. I even had to go in and hold her hand while the doctor examined her. She screamed and whimpered. When the examination was over, the doctor looked at me and shook his head. Mom had a malignant tumor in her colon. She had to take a series of cobalt radiation treatments, then have an operation that would leave her wearing a bag to hold her excrement. Leaving the doctor's office, I walked a little ahead to explain to my brother what was said in the office. When we turned around, my mother was leaning against a wall, hands cupped over her face, sobbing.

After a few weeks of cobalt and false hope, she was ready for surgery. She had wanted to beat the cancer on her own. She convinced herself that the cobalt could shrink the tumor to a size so small that she could avoid the operation. Of course, that didn't happen. It was up to me to keep Mom laughing and believing that the operation was a simple one the doctors performed every day. I told her she would be fine and up and about in no time. When I went home at night to David, I'd cry my eyes out. I had to spend eight hours a day making Mom laugh, even though I knew she was going to die. I was tense with my family. I just couldn't laugh after faking it all day.

The day of the operation came. The doctors said it was a success. They said they got "most" of the cancer, which really meant that the rest was rapidly spreading through her body. It spread to her liver, up to her breasts, then finally to her brain. She was given chemotherapy, which left her bald and blind. The last night I saw her alive, I had a belly-dance party. It was some guy's birthday, and I was hired to dance for him. It was hard to dance and look alluring while I was thinking about visiting my mother at the hospital after my show. I wouldn't have done the job, but money was tight and we really needed it. I ran through the dim corridors of the hospital in full belly-dancer makeup. It was 11:30 at night, but I was allowed in because my mother was on the critical list. When the elevator doors opened, I heard my mother screaming in pain. She was calling my name and asking me to help her.

When I got to her room, I found her with a rosary entwined on each wrist. She was a sixty-pound skeleton with huge black bruises all over her body and was bald except for a few wisps of gray hair. She had black circles under her eyes and sores in her mouth. She smelled awful. She was blind, but she knew it was me. She begged me to take her home. She wanted to be home with the family for Thanksgiving, which was the following week. In a choked voice, I told her she would be home for Thanksgiving.

I kissed her goodbye. As I left, she grabbed my arm and dug her boney fingers into it and said, "I love you." I ran out of the hospital, tears streaming down my face. My mom died that night.

Pop's response was to start drinking again. He had been sober for fourteen years. I asked him to move in with us, but I couldn't stop him from killing himself.

Go-Go

When I met David he was a very successful man. He made good money in his own business, which he shared with a partner. Things were going smoothly until one day, disaster struck. David's partner screwed the IRS for a large sum of money, screwed the employees out of pay, and then took off to parts unknown, leaving David holding the bag. After we paid the employees out of our own bank account, we started paying back the IRS. The country was in the middle of an economic crisis, work was hard to find, and David, with all his college degrees, was forced to work at menial, low-paying jobs.

We moved into a low-rent apartment on top of a bar, and making ends meet was next to impossible. Our refrigerator died, and we couldn't afford a new one. We had to eat things that didn't need to be refrigerated. My father came to the rescue. He let us use his credit card to get a new refrigerator. We had to pay him back a little each week.

Next, our car went. David had to walk to work. We asked my father for a loan so we could get a good second-hand car. He said no, but offered us his old, beat-up lemon of a car. He couldn't drive it anymore because he had a bad heart. We gratefully took the car.

We lived a dismal life, but we always made sure the kids didn't feel the tightening of our belts. We planned a big Halloween party for the kids and acted as if all was well. The children couldn't wait for David to come home so we could start the festivities. David came home all right. His face was white and his lips gray. The recession had cost him and a few others their jobs. They were all let go. "Happy Halloween."

David tried to find work elsewhere, but no one was hiring. Now what were we going to do? Bills were piling up, and the IRS was taking no excuses. We were having trouble with the car, and it was costing us plenty. Then our landlord raised the rent. Something had to be done. I knew there was good money in go-go dancing if you worked hard. With David barely able to scrape up a pittance with the jobs he could get at the moment, I thought maybe I should see what I could do. I suggested a turnaround. I would get jobs go-go dancing, and he would stay home and take care of the house and kids—until he could find a decent-paying job. David agreed the very next day.

I called up a go-go bar and was told to come down for an audition. When I hung up, I was full of bravado, but in fact I was terrified! What was I doing? Was I going to be a laughingstock? I didn't have a costume, but I did have a bikini, so I packed it in a traveling bag with a pair of high heels, and we were off to the audition. As David parked the car, my heart jumped so far up into my throat I was afraid it would pop out if I talked.

We walked down thick, red-carpeted stairs into a cool, damp bar. The stage was behind the bar and completely surrounded in blue mirrors and blue lights. It was beautiful. It was early. There were only one or two men seated at the bar. The bar owner was nice. "Anytime you're ready," he said. I went to the ladies room to change. There I met one of the dancers for that night. She was not what I expected—not very pretty, with bad skin she covered in thick, orangey makeup. She stripped right in front of me. Her breasts were long and lined with stretch marks. Even her rear end was lined. She changed into a crocheted bikini and silver high heels. She asked me if this was my first time dancing. I said, "Yes," then added, "Well, I haven't danced in a long time." She gave me a few pointers. "First, never tell anyone that you're new to dancing. They'll take advantage of you, and other dancers will tell you what to do. The men at the bar will look for flaws and give you their expert advice. The barmaids will eat you alive. Go out there and act like you've been doing this all your life. Then they'll leave you alone."

When I walked out of the bathroom, the empty bar had suddenly become packed. David sat in a corner of the bar with a nervous smile. I wore a black shirt over my costume. I bravely walked through the crowd of men to the jukebox and selected my songs. The music started. It was loud and moving. I walked behind the bar with false arrogance. I looked all the patrons in the eyes and gave the bitchy barmaid a stare that made her look down. I acted like I knew exactly what I was doing.

Well, I guess I fooled everybody, because they loved me, and I was hired immediately. In actuality, I was so scared I broke out into a nervous sweat. I went into the back to change my clothes, and I threw up.

David was my only support. He'd work all day in the apartment, taking abuse from my father all the while, then late at night he'd get ready to come in and pick me up. He never liked this. He loved to watch me dance, but he hated the environment. He never knew what to expect. In go-go bars the dancers aren't allowed to have their husbands or boyfriends hanging around, so David pretended to be a customer and I pretended not to know him. If I got done at 2:00 A.M., I could count on David to walk in at 1:30 A.M. He'd catch my last show, and I'd let him know with a slashing motion across my throat that I was just about through. It was our not-so-secret code. He'd go out and bring the car to the front of the bar, I'd dress quickly, then run out before I was followed. Then David would drive me around the mountains, with the windows down, for a little while until I wound down. Eventually he'd take me home, run my bath, prop up my pillow, and serve me a delicious, home-cooked dinner in bed. Then, when I was through, he'd rub my aching feet until I fell asleep, which was usually very soon. I don't know how he slept. I'd twitch and jerk all night long. Perpetual dancing affects your nervous system. Dancers often keep dancing even in their sleep. It's quite common.

David would let me sleep late unless I had a noon job. He wouldn't let me touch a dish or even pour myself a glass of juice. He waited on me hand and foot. I didn't do a dish in two years of go-go dancing. When I finally tried to do the dishes again, I'd forgotten how!

I always dressed in my costume at home and threw a baggy dress on over it. This gave me options. In most bars, the ladies' room is the dressing room, and in general you can bet on the ladies' room being occupied, either by an old, fat barfly puking her guts up, another dancer primping, barmaids smoking pot, or even lesbian lovers going at it. The air usually smells like burnt pizza and sour bar rags. A sea of sweaty, flushed faces watches in anticipation as I climb the short stepladder to the small stage. Red and yellow lights blink off and on. The music is loud. I begin my first twenty-minute set of the evening. Unlike most dancers, I look the audience square in the face, establishing my supremacy right from the start. My eyes scan the bar for would-be troublemakers. I want to know where they are at all times. The dancing itself is easy for me. Many dancers take ridicule for basically not being able to dance. Sometimes you'd think we had an audience full of Fred Astaires and Gene Kellys. As I dance, I read the sign language of the patrons. Rubbing the side of one's nose means, "Do you want to buy cocaine?" or, "Do you have any cocaine?" or, "Would you like to share my cocaine?" Opening one's wallet or billfold and exposing large bills to the dancer means, "Are you free to party?" Pointing to one's watch means, "When do you get off?"

Sending a dollar or a drink up to a dancer means, "Will you sit with me on your break?" You do, of course. To refuse a drink at a go-go bar can be hazardous to your health. For one thing, the owner wants the patron to keep ordering drinks so the house makes money. You also don't want to make the patron feel you're too good for him, even though you are, so you order a drink—never a soda, the bar owner will kill you. Besides, "real men" don't buy soda, wine, or champagne. These are commonly thought to be "fag drinks." You may order a shot or a beer or both. This way, nobody gets emasculated. If all you drink is wine, well thats O.K., too, just as long as you order a shot next to it. Don't worry, you won't have to drink the shot. The patron will do that for you, just as long as it goes on record that he never bought just wine. There are, however, dancers who will match any man shot for shot. These young ladies usually end up falling off the stage. Accepting a drink from a patron often opens the door to endless, boring stories of Vietnam or World War II, depending on the patron's age.

Usually there are good dancing songs on the house jukebox, but every go-go bar has at least one dipshit song that someone keeps playing and you keep rejecting. Some songs are impossible to dance to, even for a good dancer. For instance, around Christmas the jukebox is stuffed with Christmas tunes. Now, dancing to "Jingle Bell Rock" isn't too bad, but it's impossible, even sacrilegious, to dance to "Silent Night." Once a customer played "The Star Spangled Banner." I didn't know whether to dance while saluting with my hand on one breast or what. Then there's the favorite song of the barmaid with the broken heart. Her affair with a married man has fallen through, and she keeps playing some depressing tear-jerker. You can't reject a barmaid's song—for one thing, they control the reject button. Second, they pay you at the end of the night. And, finally, they usually have a sawed-off pool stick behind the bar they can smash your toes with. You make the most of their songs.

Fighting at the end of the night for your pay is not unusual. In fact, it's common. Barmaids take their frustrations out on the dancer. If a dancer's pantyhose have a run in them, she can have her pay reduced. Same thing if she's late. If she flashes, the barmaid has the right to fire the dancer without any pay at all.

Another permanent fixture in the go-go bar is the spotter. His job is to go from bar to bar, acting like a patron, ogling the dancers, and waiting for one of them to flash. When she does, it's all over. He whips out a badge, corners the dancer, and scares the hell out of her with comments about anything from going to prison to the investigations by the IRS.

When you go for a go-go audition, there are three main things to check out: the lighting, the music, and, most important, the stage. I have danced on all kinds of stages. Once I walked into a bar that seemed to have no stage at all. When I asked the owner where I would be dancing, he said, "Up there, next to the register." He pointed to a small ledge with a rack of potato chips on it. He removed the chips and said, "Hop up." I asked if there was any lighting for me, to which he replied, "I'll open the blinds." Then there was a bar that spent a fortune on renovations. It had a big horseshoe bar with fine leather seats, video games, a television screen as big as one wall, and a fancy jukebox. The stage was another matter—a pair of sawhorses with a sheet of plywood across them, raw, unvarnished wood. The lighting was a naked blue lightbulb that dangled in your face. When you leaned against the stucco wall, you tore the ass out of your pantyhose. It was the only stage I ever danced on that bounced. You had to be careful not to dance too close to the edge, or you would bounce over the bar, headfirst. I've danced on a table, a chair, and a wooden block. One bartender told me there was no stage. "Just dance around the customers, O.K.?" No, not O.K.

One night I was dancing with an over-the-hill dancer. She was almost fifty, but she didn't want to hang it up. She had danced in the early 1960s, and she used to be quite beautiful. In her mind's eye she still was, but in reality she was overweight and doughy. She had varicose veins and a million lines in her face. The patrons called her "Go-Go Granny." She never got a break from unpleasant remarks but she plodded on. She had a twenty-two-year-old son. One night he came into the bar. The look on his face when his mother was dancing was one of disgust and pity. He looked around at the patrons, who were ribbing each other and making obscene gestures to his mother. Finally, one smartass turns to the boy, not knowing who he was, and said, "How would you like to wake up next to that old cow some morning? Imagine fucking that!" The young man's eyes welled up in tears and then he flew into a rage. He literally broke up the bar and was arrested for almost killing the guy who'd provoked him. This is a sad story, but it is not by no means an isolated one. We had many older dancers who, for various reasons, wouldn't retire gracefully.

The dancers came from many walks of life. Some were school teachers during the day and go-go girls by night. One dancer taught first grade. One night she attended an early evening PTA meeting, then went dancing for dollars. In walked two of the fathers she had just spoken to at the PTA meeting. Well, they sat half the night with the teacher, buying her drinks and so on. When they tried to clap her erasers, she refused to play ball, so the two honest citizens of the PTA felt it their duty to report her to the Board of Education. She was fired, of course. Talk about hypocrisy. No one ever asked these solid citizens just what they were doing in a go-go joint in the first place.

Another dancer I knew was a tiny thing, very frail except for a size 44D chest! When she walked she looked top-heavy, like she was leaning forward. Nature had not been that kind to her, however. These were super-deluxe implants. The girl used to complain how much they hurt. I once asked her why she had gotten such big knockers. Why not medium-sized ones? It seems her husband, who'd married her when she was a 32A, insisted on it. He loved big tits. His mother had big tits. If she didn't want to lose him, she had better get the implants. Like a fool, she agreed. She even had to pay for them herself. Later I found out he left her for a skinny chick with no tits at all.

Every bar has its "masseur." This is a chap who wants nothing better than to get his sweaty little hands on a dancer. Now these guys aren't dumb. Any dancer, young, middle-aged, or old, loves to get her aching feet rubbed or her neck massaged. These men will even buy you a drink for the privilege. Yes, I fell for this. I even looked forward to seeing one of my masseurs, but then, so did all the other dancers. These guys knew exactly what they were doing, and consequently got all the dancers. It was the only thing we had to look forward to, except going home.

Every bar usually has its photographer also. He holds out his hands and frames your face in an imaginary lens. "Hold it," "Perfect!" "You'd be perfect for a magazine spread I'm doing," "You're going to be Miss April," "Would you be interested in posing for *Playboy*?"

"We can do the photos tonight after you get done dancing, at my apartment." This ploy had little effect on me. With my experience working for men's magazines, I knew a lot about photo shoots— enough to know that you don't pluck a model out of a go-go bar for a photo session at three o'clock in the morning after she's been dancing all night and has swollen feet and dark circles under her eyes. I also knew, of course, that it is next to impossible to get into *Playboy,* no matter how beautiful you are. I don't think they use models; I think they grow their own girls in a garden behind the Playboy Mansion.

One time I thought I'd have some fun with Mr. Snapshot. I asked him what kind of lighting he used, to which he nervously replied, "I have a box of flash cubes." I asked, "What kind of backdrop do you use?" He replied, "I nail a red blanket to the wall. But if you would rather, I also have a black satin sheet." So much for my shot in *Playboy.*

A lot of bars also have a CIA agent in residence. He's not supposed to tell you this, but this may be his last night on earth. Enemy agents are tracking him down. The government wants to put him on an island, all expenses paid, for the rest of his life, but he can't ever leave the island. He knows too many top secrets. "I saw that program, too."

Finally, there are the college students writing papers on sleaze. They breeze in with their preppy friends and their girlfriends. The girls clutch tightly at their Annie Hall layered-look outfits, as though anyone gives a damn about them when there are half-naked dancers and hookers in tight pink, satin hotpants all over the place. The guys buy you a drink then start asking dumbass questions like, "Does dancing turn you on? Are you an exhibitionist? Do you pay taxes on this?" Some of these pencilnecks brought tape recorders with them. One dancer took a tape recorder's microphone, spewed a string of obscenities into it, then dropped the mike into the preppy's beer.

Bar hustlers are a common sight in go-go clubs. They're salesmen who sell lovely (and expensive) costumes to the dancers. They were hard to resist, but I never bought one thing from them. I saw girls go into terrible debt for costumes. Sometimes they turned their entire pay over to a hustler, meaning they danced for nothing. One hustler was a slippery character called Gold Bug. This fellow had the finest gold jewelry you could imagine, very cheap. He did a thriving business. I couldn't imagine turning over money I literally sweat for to get costumes or jewelry. My money was buying me my freedom, so I stayed clear of the hustlers.

There was one exception, however. One day around Christmas, I was up on stage dancing when in walked a tall young man with an armful of wrench sets. He walked up and down the bar, hustling the customers. Nobody bought one. They were too busy gaping at me. A couple of guys who had been pains in the ass all day sat directly in front of the stage, so I could hear everything they said. When the wrench salesman approached them, they ridiculed him, to which he responded, "You could have just said no. I'm trying to get some money together for Christmas, that's all." I felt bad about it. I watched the young man gather up his wrench sets and start to leave. Suddenly, I don't know what hit me, I yelled out, "Wait! I'll take a wrench set." I came down from the stage and walked over to the young man, who looked down at me with suspicious eyes. I offered him six dollars for a wrench set. He said, "You can have one for free," but I insisted he take the money. He said, "You don't really want a wrench set do you?" I told him, "No, but I understand what it's like to hustle in a bar and be humiliated. So take the money and maybe someday you can help me out."

After that, he became a friend. He got another job and was doing alright. Every time he would see me dancing somewhere, he'd tip me five dollars and buy me a drink. I always felt safe when he was in a bar where I was dancing. He was very protective of me.

A lot of go-go customers have "fallen in love" with me. Some were nice and very sincere, but usually they just wanted to date a dancer. The conversation usually went, "What is a nice girl like you doing in a job like this? Let me take you away from all this." One guy even told me we could live above his parents' garage. He made good money, almost $200 a week. I didn't want to hurt his feelings, but I made more than that in one night.

There were intriguing barmaids in every bar. One bar had a very fat, homely barmaid who weighed about three hundred pounds. She had very large, flabby breasts she loved to display by wearing low-cut dresses or blouses. She was very horny at all times. When men would order a beer, she'd proposition them. If their hands were cold, she'd grab them and shove them down her cleavage. For a real treat, she would look some poor guy straight in the eye, then whip out a huge tit and lay it on the bar. It would spread out like melting ice cream, covering the bar. She thought this was a sexy come-on. To most men, it meant going on the wagon. Once when I was on my break I sat down at the bar to have a piece of "bar pizza" (burned to a cinder). No one was on the stage yet. My partner was still getting dressed when, slowly and methodically, the fat barmaid slithered up on the stage and started to strip, looking very sensually at the horrified patrons. She lay on her back and did floor work, raising her ham legs up over her head and exposing mounds of white, stretch-marked flab. A tiny Puerto Rican guy in the audience went berserk at this display. He jumped over the bar and landed on this human beach ball. She wrapped her legs around him and almost broke his back. Fortunately for him, the owner broke it up. Everyone drank in silence for the rest of the night.

Another curious barmaid was a girl about thirty-four, pretty, but tall and awkwardly built. In the beginning of the evening she was always quiet, but she would drink Southern Comfort (steadily), and by the middle of the evening she would be wasted. If a guy asked her for a bottle of beer, she would do a little dance in front of him, rolling her tongue in and out before she gave it to him. Then she'd walk up and down the bar taking sips from everyone's beer bottles. No one said anything to her because she frightened them. This barmaid had the additional characteristic of being absent-minded. On New Year's Eve, the busiest night of the year for all bars, she suddenly discovered that she had forgotten to hire a dancer. Now it was New Year's Eve, and all dancers working that night were already booked. I never worked on New Year's Eve. The phone rang. It was the absent-minded barmaid begging me to come in. The money is exceptionally good New Year's Eve, but I had to refuse since it is also the most dangerous night to be go-go dancing. The barmaid was fired.

I'm not exaggerating when I say New Year's Eve is a dangerous night to dance. I've heard many terrible stories. One dancer was dancing to a crowded New Year's Eve audience, when suddenly some wiseass threw a cherry bomb at her. It shattered the three big mirrors that surrounded her on stage, sending razor-sharp shards of blue glass into her face. Blood covered the stage. The dancer was taken out in an ambulance. She was blinded in one eye for life. With her other eye, she could see a deep scar left on her cheek.

Another bar had a group of studs who heckled dancers by yelling, "Take it off!" One girl refused, so the bastards locked the front door, tore off the dancer's clothes, and took turns raping her on the pool table. Then they threw her in the back alley next to all the garbage cans. She also never got paid. At another bar on New Year's Eve there was a young couple in the audience. The husband was making overtures toward the dancer, and his wife was getting jealous. All night her husband threw money at the dancer and compared his wife to her unfavorably. The wife drank steadily. Finally, she got sick and ran into the ladies' room, which doubled as a storage room. While on her knees next to the toilet she noticed a lye solution the bar used for killing mice and rats. She brought it back into the bar with her. She said later that she was only planning to scare her husband with it, but when she caught him talking to the pretty young dancer on her break, she let it fly in the girl's face. The dancer's skin literally started to melt down her face. I heard that she killed herself a few months later. On another New Year's Eve night, a go-go bar was held up by men in ski masks. Everyone in the bar was told to lie face down on the floor. The dancer was told to lie face down on the stage. The men robbed the register, the dancer looked up, and the men shot and killed both the bartender and dancer for it.

Another bad time to work in go-go bars is any night of a full moon. I know this sounds ridiculous, but it is nevertheless true. I was never one to believe in superstitions, so I had to find out from experience. Bar people go absolutely bonkers the night of a full moon. Fights break out for no apparent reason, paranoia is in full swing, and dancers are treated terribly. One night of a full moon, the men were obnoxious and cheap to me. I hardly made any tips at all. The barmaid was fighting with her boyfriend in the back kitchen, and he slapped her so hard I could hear the crack all the way up on stage. A customer pulled a fast one with the other barmaid. He claimed he'd given her a twenty-dollar bill, when in fact he'd given her a five. This is a common trick when the bar is busy. This caused a ruckus between the owner, the barmaid, and the patron. In order to keep the customer, the owner refunded the patron's change from the twenty, promptly took it out of the barmaid's pay, causing her to quit on the spot, forcing the dancer I was dancing with to tend bar as well as dance, and forcing me to dance longer and more sets. Later in the evening, the barmaid brought her burly boyfriend in to take care of the bar owner, causing six guys with pool sticks to beat the boyfriend to a pulp, causing the police to come. To cap the evening, a guy with a brown, bushy beard and long wild hair jumped up on the pool table, tore open his shirt, and yelled, "I am the Wolfman!"

Every go-go bar has a town idiot employed to be a gofer or do all the bar's dirty work. One such bar had a six-foot-three guy called Willy filling the role. Willy was about thirty-seven, had no teeth, and his eyes were four inches apart. He'd been in and out of mental institutions for most of his life. His job in the bar was to go shopping for toilet paper, maintain the filthy bathrooms, and clean up the mess if someone puked. He was cheap labor and very often taken advantage of. Once, he walked around to everyone in the crowded bar, tapping them on the shoulders and telling them that he was insane, and that he had the papers to prove it. Then he would pull out a legal document that did indeed say he was insane. He wasn't allowed to drink in the bar, as there was no telling what he'd do when he was drunk. There was a song on the jukebox that exercised him, "Coward of the County." Once when he heard the song he threw pool balls at people, turned over the pool table, and knocked everyone's drink off the bar.

It took about ten men to subdue him. Still, people regularly played the song to get him going. Willy liked to perform. His favorite act was standing on his head on stage. This was very humorous, especially when all the change fell out of his pockets. Once the owner dared Willy to put on an old, black-lace shortie nightie and dance on stage. Willy went to the bathroom, stripped down, got into the nightie, and jumped on stage with just the nightie on and his long, bony, hairy legs stuck into his sneakers. He started dancing and the bar went wild. Just as Willy was executing a high kick, the door opened up and in walked a few guys from out of town. The looks on their faces were priceless. Without taking his hand off the doorknob, the one guy said to his pals, "I didn't know it was this type of place, honest." In another bar, there was a pair of village idiots. One was a dapper, eighty-year-old man. He always wore a suit and a snazzy bowtie. His job was to run for coffee and sandwiches for the barmaids and dancers. He used to talk endlessly about his many conquests of women. His pal was a slow guy with a hook for a hand. His problem was that he was fifty years old and still a virgin. The two used to fight like hell in the bar. The old stud used to say, "You should be ashamed of yourself!" Then Captain Hook would cry. This happened every day. One of the regulars in this particular bar was an old jerk who faithfully watched every go-go girl, then prayed out loud for their souls, "Forgive them, Father, for they know not what they are doing." It turned out he used to be a big-time whoremaster and then he got religion. Suddenly it was his mission to save wayward women. But, in order to pray for us, he felt it his duty to check us out first, so he knew whom to pray for.

You'll find a hero in almost every go-go bar, someone who will protect you if necessary. One bar had a mountain man for a customer. He popped down into civilization only twice a year. He lived on bear meat and looked the part. He was about six-foot-eight and probably weighed close to three hundred pounds. He had a thick, wildass, reddish-brown beard. He idolized women and was particularly fond of me. He tipped me twenty dollars after each show from money he got selling animal pelts.

Once I was dancing when the mountain man was in the audience. Next to him was a yuppie, small and tweedy with wire-framed glasses. Well, he got loaded and started yelling wiseass remarks at me. Then he turned to the mountain man and said, "I just love busting on women," to which the mountain man replied, after grabbing the yuppie by his tweed lapels and lifting him off his seat, "I just *love* women!"

The bouncers in go-go bars are almost nonexistent, and the dancer usually has to fend for herself. Some bars, however, have hidden bouncers who get paid off in drinks. These men are built like walking cinder blocks. One guy was tall and husky, had a light blond beard, and kept to himself. He like to watch me dance to one particular country western song. He was so sensitive that my dancing brought tears to his eyes. He would play his tune over and over again. The song was about a broken-down go-go girl still trying to make it. I didn't just dance to it, I played the part. One night while I was enacting this song for him, a troublemaker started a fight. Without taking his eyes off of me, this gentle giant went over to the loudmouth and socked him so hard in the stomach that the guy folded like a card table. Then, by the scruff of the neck, he threw the jerk into the street—all before the song was over. He finished in time to clap for my performance.

The regulars in go-go bars know the rules and rarely make trouble. The go-go bar is their home away from home. Some even get their mail sent to the bar. It's the outsiders who start all the problems. Getting thrown out into the streets by the scruff of your pants is not something you only see in the movies. I've seen it done countless times. I have even had to quickly jump out of the way of the door while someone got the heave-ho. It's an unwritten rule, but everyone seems to be in agreement. The people congregating nearest the door watch very carefully when there's a brawl anywhere in the bar. This usually occurs around the pool table. If the bouncer grabs the collar and the seat of the troublemaker's pants, then the people near the door clear a path, and the bouncer runs the guy out with the speed and strength of a locomotive; hence, the expression "bum's rush." If you don't believe me, try hanging out in a go-go bar on a Friday night with a full moon. On nights like that they don't bother to close the door.

Barroom employees and the best regulars make a little world all their own. It's an unpretentious world of country western music, fighting, breaking up, and making up. All these elements can be seen in a barroom wedding. It usually goes something like this: A barmaid who's divorced her third husband remarries her first husband. Her maid of honor is his second ex-wife. The best man is the ex-husband she just divorced. There's a passel of kids between them and they're one big, happy family until the end of the evening, when everyone is shit-faced. I don't mean mellow—I mean shit-faced. First there's the wedding, sometime in the early afternoon. The groom has been in the bar since before it opened, tuxedo and all. The bride has been at the beauty parlor. After the wedding, everybody moves to the reception, held at the go-go bar, of course. White streamers and paper wedding bells hang everywhere. Congratulations are spray painted on the stage mirrors. The door bursts open and the wedding party walks in. The women look beautiful in their long, flowing gowns, with flowers woven into their hair. The men are handsome in their tuxedos. They're the same men who are at the bar night after night in plaid shirts and baseball caps. They've even shaved. Drinks are passed around. Not champagne (that's for fags), but "Alabama Slammers," "Kamikazis," and "Harvey Wallbangers." And that's just for the women. The men drink only shots and beer. They dance to country western music, have wedding photos taken in front of such memorable things as the jukebox, the pool table, or the door that says "Gents." There's something priceless about a women all dressed up in a flowing, feminine wedding gown leaning over a pool table, getting ready to break.

All these ex's getting along so well always ends up too good to be true. After drinking all night, at least one girl in a long gown is hugging the toilet, a couple of guys are passed out on the pool table, kids are jamming up the jukebox, and, finally, there's the bride crying, black mascara running down her lined face. She starts tend-ing bar in her bridal gown. The groom is flirting with his second wife, and now the bride remembers why she divorced him in the first place. One of the drunken bridesmaids decides to jump up on the stage and try to outdo the go-go girl. She hikes up her gown to expose baggy, tan pantyhose and a long-leg girdle. Getting dizzy, she staggers down from the stage and pukes behind the bar. Finally the air-conditioner goes and hell on earth is complete. The bride leaves with her sisters, and the groom falls asleep in his pickup truck, streamers still hanging from it. The next night everybody is lovey dovey again and the beat goes on. This is a true story.

The bars I worked in had their share of degenerates as well. One such person was a guy who was about forty-five and well-dressed; he held a respectable job. He came in often and liked to talk to me. He was very nice, never once putting the make on me, and very generous with tips. But one day he asked me about my children. He was particularly interested in my four-year-old daughter, Juliet. He asked to see a picture of her. I thought nothing of it, so I showed him a photo of my little angel. He was intrigued by the picture and asked me if he could keep it. I didn't know what to do. This was an unusual request even for a go-go bar. I had to say no. Then he asked me if I would let him take Juliet out on a date to Chuck E. Cheese, a kiddie-type restaurant. Just the two of them, he forty-five and she four years old! I was speechless! He showed me a photo of a girl he was dating at the time. She was all of eight years old! He assured me that the girl's mother had given him the photo as well as permission to see her. "You see," he said, "I love younger women."

We had a man, about fifty, come in all the time and bring his wife and his little grandson, who was about seven. The man said he wanted to make sure his grandson didn't grow up to be gay, so he was going to teach him early how to be a man. He taught the kid how to play pool. The kid got pretty good. He taught the kid how to screw the jukebox out of a quarter and still get your song. He also taught this future little macho taco how to swear like a sailor and heckle go-go girls. While I was dancing, the kid would yell up, very loudly, "You've got an ass like a truck," or "Are those your real tits?" or "Bend over and crack a smile." He would throw balled-up, wet cocktail napkins at me. Once, when I was sitting down on my break, he came up and dropped an ice cube down my bra. This brought peels of laughter from his proud grandparents. In case you're wondering why the grandparents were watching baby Franken-stein so much, both his parents were in jail for dealing drugs.

Bar kids are a sad breed unto their own. I will never bring my children into a bar. Some barmaids brought their kids to work with them. I'd see these poor kids trying to do their homework in some corner with swearing, loud music, loud talking, and fist-fights all around them. They ate microwave pizza for dinner and all the soda they wanted, potato chips for a side order and beer nuts for dessert. When they were bored, they would watch endless sports on the television sets that hung from the ceiling. People made endless jokes about them watching the go-go girls. These kids were usually full of resentment and tried to ignore their mothers.

I heard the news when I got to work one day. Sherry had been found by two Boy Scouts in a wooded area, nude and badly decom-posed. Sherry had been a very beautiful dancer—tall, blonde, and twenty-three. Everyone liked her. She was friendly to all. Weeks before her death she'd been complaining that someone was following her when she drove home late at night after work. She had been stabbed in the stomach and the top of her head was gone.

Chills ran down my spine as I got the details from the bar owner. He'd had to go down to the morgue to identify her. How could I dance after hearing this? Who could have done it? Maybe it was a steady customer. Was this going to be open season on go-go dancers?

As time went by, go-go girls got increasingly nervous about the killer on the loose, and many girls quit their bookings, so work was abundant for me. One night, a few weeks later, I was finding it espe-cially difficult going to work. Getting ready for a night job was a drag in any case. When most people were settling down for the night with a good television movie, I was getting ready to blast off to the go-go bar and who knows what. Standing in front of my dresser mirror, costumes for the night spread out on the bed, I couldn't help thinking about Sherry. I pinned my pantyhose to my G-string and wondered just how safe dancing was. My bag was packed and I was off.

This particular night the bar was crowded, standing room only. The hoots, howls, and wild laughing could mean only one thing— there was a flasher on stage. Great. She'd probably been giving the audience peep shows all afternoon and getting them all riled up. I was going to take over, and all they were going to get from me was dancing. I'd have to handle nasty, drunken remarks and make the best of it until 2:30 A.M. I knew it was going to be a rough night when I saw a tall guy at the bar dressed in a full-body rabbit costume complete with a huge rabbit head and floppy ears. Most nights I immediately pushed past the crowd of imbeciles and went to the closet known as the ladies' room. It also doubled as our dressing room. It consisted of a dirty toilet, dirtier sayings written on the wall, a long, smudgy mirror with curious lipstick kisses all over it, and (of course) no toilet paper. One of the other dancers was in the ladies' room changing already. She was not very pretty but she had a good body. All the guys took advantage of her, then abused her. They would ridicule her in front of the whole bar. Later that evening she was having a drink at the bar, minding her own business, when some guys decided to humiliate her. They shouted across the bar that she should put a paper bag over her head because she was hurting their eyes. They even supplied the paper bag with two holes cut out for eyes. She was a good sport about it and slipped the bag on her head while she sat at the bar, but I could see that under that bag tears ran down her cheeks in silence. When she went to the ladies' room a little later, the guys locked her in. She pounded maniacally on the door, pleading to get out. They knew she was claustrophobic, but this was great fun. I couldn't stand to watch this form of torture for long, so after a minute I ran and let her out. Her eyes were wild and her face was all covered in sweat as she gasped for air. I wasn't too popular that night, but I was stronger.

Sherry's murderer was finally found one day. It was her old boyfriend. He'd been ticked off because she broke up with him, so he said if he couldn't have her, no one else would. Sherry's parents refused to claim her body, so she was buried in a pauper's grave. She was just another whore, good riddance. Dancers are just pieces of interchangeable meat. Oh, sure, everyone is fascinated by them, but, if one should die, who cares? It's not like it was a good girl. My father was a perfect example of someone with this all-American attitude. When Mom died he very seriously said, "Why your mother? She was such a good woman, and to think of those whores out there still living. Why couldn't it have been one of them?" When I informed Pop that a "whore" can feel the agony of cancer, too, he told me, "Yes, but they deserve it." That's a common attitude towards dancers. We aren't supposed to have any feelings.

Many people think that go-go girls are usually prostitutes. This is not the case. A few are, but I could count the ones I knew on one hand. A night didn't go by that I didn't get propositioned by someone. Most men backed off when I told them that pay sex was not my thing, but a few were downright rude about it. They insisted that all dancers sold their bodies and we all had a price. What, they demanded, was mine? Once, while changing my costume in the ladies' room, the barmaid came in and handed me a thousand-dollar bill! She said it was mine if I cared to go home with a Japanese gentleman out front. The whole bar knew what was going on. You could hear a pin drop out there while the barmaid was talking to me. I was doing my makeup. I looked at the bill, touched it to see what it felt like (it felt good), then sent it back to the gentleman with a "Thanks, but no thanks." The barmaid thought I was a fool, but everyone in the bar had much-increased respect for me after that.

I've encountered some ghoulish things in go-go bars. Once two young dancers were found murdered. They had been missing from the go-go circuit for a couple of weeks. I didn't know them. I only heard about it from other dancers. They had been seen leaving a bar with a strange-looking man. Later, they were found in a motel room, stabbed to death.

Well, soon after I met a strange-looking man in a redneck bar I was dancing in. All the guys in this bar wore jeans, plaid shirts or t-shirts, wallets chained to their pants, and peaked caps that said "Budweiser" on them. They were shooting pool, playing Pac Man, and arm wrestling when a man about thirty or so walked in, tall, thin, and dressed in an immaculate black suit with a crisp white shirt and black tie. His hair was neither short nor long, and it was blue-black. His eyebrows were thick and black, and his skin was extremely white, smooth, and flawless. He wore a black, drooping mustache. His eyes were piercing black, and his lips were dead purple, like when someone gets cold. He walked quietly through the rednecks and took a seat at a table. He ordered a burgundy wine and sipped it while he watched me and my partner dance. Strangely enough, none of the rednecks bothered him. This was highly unusual, he being a stranger and looking so weird. They bothered everyone who was out of the ordinary, but not him. On my break, the man asked me to join him for a drink. When he looked at me, his eyes seemed to burn right through my brain. He brushed my long hair off of my neck, then, very gently, touched it. He remarked with fascination how lovely and white my skin was. He kept staring at my neck. I felt very strange and didn't want to stay any longer than I had to. During my next set he left with a regular bar hooker, but, before they went out the door, he looked up at me one more time with those burning eyes. Then he smiled and left. I don't know what happened to the hooker, but I never saw her again. Someone said she got arrested. Somebody else said she got married. I wonder.

One of my trademarks was a leather, spike-studded wristband I wore every time I danced. This was purely for protection. I wore it loose, so at any time I could slide it down and use it as brass knuckles. Many patrons were turned off by the bracelet. They thought I was a biker chick or into sadomasochism or just being a smartass. I didn't let that worry me. It was a simple safety precaution.

One night I was dancing at a well-known flasher bar. The patrons were used to seeing obscene acts, so when I came on that night and only danced I got a lot of verbal abuse. Now, verbal abuse I can

Right: Yvette Paris's mother, Agnes Marie Baker. *Bottom left:* Yvette as toddler: Barbara Ann Baker at three years old. *Bottom right:* Yvette with her father, Jacob Frank Baker (Westy), and her brother, Jack.

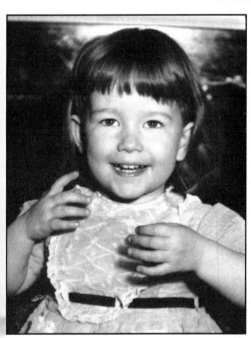

Yvette in high school: age 17; *inset:* age 14.

Yvette with her first husband, Jim Lambert. *Inset:* Yvette with her son Jack in Florida.

Top left: Yvette the belly dancer. *(Photo by Bill Swanson.) Top right:* Yvette wearing her infamous leather-studded bracelet. *(Photo by Bill Swanson.) Bottom:* Yvette bending over backwards to please her audience. *(Photo by James Kriegsmann, Jr.)*

A coy Yvette on St. Patrick's Day. *(Photo by Bill Swanson.)*

Yvette all dolled up as Marilyn, with David's support before Joe Franklin's Marilyn Monroe lookalike contest. *Inset:* Yvette with her husband and manager, David March. *(Photo by Annie Sprinkle.)*

Top left: Yvette's stepson, Jimmy Lambert. *(Photo by James Lambert.) Top right:* The family relaxing: David, Yvette, Juliet, and Jack. *(Photo by James Lambert.) Bottom:* Juliet and Yvette with Mickey Mouse at Disney World. *(Photo by David March.)*

Top: Yvette with Sally Jessy Raphael after her appearance on the "Sally Jessy Raphael Show." *(Photo by David March.)* *Bottom left:* David and Yvette with Bob Rosen, Editor of *D-Cup* magazine. *(Photo by Jack Lambert.) Bottom right:* Yvette with exotic world notables Al Goldstein, Publisher of *Screw* magazine, and Xaviera Hollander, "The Happy Hooker." *(Photo by David March.)*

Top left: Burlesque Queens *(from left to right):* Yvette Paris, Jennie Lee, and Ann Corio. *(Photo by David March.) Top right:* Striptease stars of today *(from left to right):* Suzie Boobies, Ebony, and Yvette Paris. *(Photo by David March.) Bottom:* A strippers reunion in Times Square, 1989. Striptease artists *(from left to right):* Ann Corio, Bambi Vawn, Leola Harlow, Jennie Lee, and Yvette Paris with adult-film star, Annie Sprinkle. *(Photo by David March.)*

Top left: Yvette with her Golden Fanny Award. *(Photo by James Lambert.) Top right:* Yvette as Jean Harlow. *(Photo by James Kriegsmann, Jr.) Bottom:* Yvette posing for *Iron Horse* magazine. (Photo by Bill Swanson.)

Top right: Yvette's first time on stage at Bob Anthony's Harmony Theatre, where she was first dubbed the "Queen of Burlesque." *(Photo by Dominique.) Bottom left: Photo by Neil Wexler. Bottom right: Photo by Dominique.*

(Photo by Dominique.)

handle—but don't get physical, I'm never in the mood for it. While I was on the stage, some loud little pain in the ass kept yelling up for me to take my top off. He was short, about forty-five, with a ski hat pulled over his silly-ass face. I shook my head no. When I was on my break, I went to the jukebox to study the songs. As this was a new bar for me, I wanted to get used to the numbers. Well, the little weasel walked up to me and said, "You're only kidding about not flashing, right?" I told him I was not kidding. He got angry. He said, "Maybe I should take you in the back room and knock you around a little. Then you'd flash!" I have a vile O'Leary temper and my blood started to boil, but I kept things under control. Starting a fight in a go-go bar is not wise. I just glared at the lowlife, then pushed past him to the stage for my next set.

Before long I heard the little bastard yelling, "Take it the fuck off!" I ignored him, but I wasn't sure how long I could maintain my discipline. The stage was surrounded in mirrors, and, when I turned around, in the corner of my eye I caught the jerk aiming a beer bottle at me. That was it. I snapped. I whirled around, jumped off the stage, and grabbed his wrist before he could let the bottle fly. With his other hand, he slapped me hard across the side of my head, making my ears ring. I promptly knocked him down. In a second I found myself rolling around the floor with the idiot. I must have been a sight in my red-sequined costume. At my first chance, I pulled the studded bracelet around my fist and pounded the shit out of the jerk's face. Two bouncers had to pull me off of him. They took me, kicking and screaming, up the four short steps to the ladies' room and told me to stay there and cool down. I did, but in a minute, I heard the little asshole shouting up the steps for me to come back so he could finish me. The bouncers told him to quiet down and have a beer on the house. "All right," he yelled, "but she better get her shit together or I'll knock the piss out of her!"

What can I say? I'll only be pushed so far. I jumped up, almost tore the door off the ladies' room, and started round two. I literally leapt from the top of the stairs and landed square on top of the bigmouth. We both went down with a thud. I then pounded my bracelet so hard into his face that I had to twist it to get the studs out. From now on, every time he shaves he'll think of me and my studded bracelet.

We had a number of would-be bikers (insurance agents on their days off) come in and play Hud. Now, a real biker will only ride a Harley Davidson motorcycle, but would-be's just out trying to be cool ride Yamahas or Hondas. They would storm into various go-go bars like John Wayne, wearing shades and leather jackets, only they were clean-shaven and had close-cropped hair (but styled). These people usually rolled in on a Saturday. They were obnoxious to the barmaids and the dancers. One particularly hot day, I was dancing in a "real" bikers' hangout. It was early and no bikers had come in yet. The air-conditioner had broken down, making dancing next to impossible. When I got done dancing for my twenty minutes, I was saturated in perspiration, my hair was as wet as if I'd just stepped out of the shower, and the sequins on my bra were soaked and very irritating. It had to be over a hundred degrees in that sweatbox. I was getting dizzy from the lack of oxygen and the smoke filling the room. In walked the insurance agency's answer to the Hell's Angels. They peeled off their shades and leather-studded gloves, then started in making snide remarks to the barmaid. Soon they zeroed in on me. One guy kept yelling that sweaty girls turned him off and that I should go dry off so he could enjoy his drink. Then another yelled, "When's the dancer coming on?" Next they start harassing me to take off my costume bra. I was getting dizzy and had to turn around and lean on the mirrored wall. I closed my eyes and wished to God my biker friends would walk in. Just when I thought I'd faint, just as they had started yelling, "Take it off, slut," I heard a loud bang. I opened my eyes and saw in the mirror nine of the sweatiest, hairiest, most tattooed bikers imaginable. If you were casting for Hell's Angels, these would be your boys. They were the regulars, who, believe it or not, never hassled the dancers or barmaids. In fact, they treated me very nicely. They even wrote prison poetry to me. The bikers stood around watching the insurance men hassle me. Suddenly one yelled out, "Who owns those Mickey Mouse bikes out front?" Another biker yelled out to the one telling me to take off my bra, "If she does, you're dead." One of the would-be bikers went out to check their Hondas, only to find that they were all knocked over and on top of one another in the gutter. My biker friends escorted them out of the bar. That's putting it mildly. Let's just say we were never bothered by them again.

One jerkwater little bar was owned by the slipperiest little owner. His name was Sal. He cheated the dancers every chance he got. God forbid your foot left the stage one minute before your twenty minutes were up. He'd deduct a dollar from your pay. He hated laughter. Because he was so short, he always thought people were laughing at him, so you weren't allowed to laugh in his bar. One night he was in the back room counting money when I was on stage. I started kidding with some of the regulars. We were all having fun. One of the guys had an infectious laugh and got the whole bar roaring with laughter. Suddenly, out stormed little Sal in baggy pants, hands on hips. "Who's laughing?" he demanded. "Anyone who laughs can get the hell out!"

Sal was the original Scrooge. He paid the dancers less than any other bar-owner and then demanded more time out of them. Our first set lasted one hour as opposed to the usual twenty minutes. It is *very* exhausting to dance nonstop for an hour. He screwed me once, too. He asked me to work Thanksgiving night and said he'd pay me double because it was a holiday. Plus, the bar would be packed and I'd make a lot in tips. I *never* work on holidays, but I really needed the money and he made the offer so attractive I couldn't say no. Christmas was coming and I could get the kids some really good things with the extra money. So, after cooking a big dinner and enjoying a comfortable day with my family, I had go-go dancing to look forward to. I packed my bag, said goodbye to the kids, and set off. When I got there, the bar was empty except for a bartender. I sat at the bar in full costume with sequins and straight pins jabbing me in the ass. It was time to get up and dance, but for whom? I stayed put. In walked another dancer attracted by the double-pay offer. She got in full costume and joined me at the bar.

I was drinking club soda but she was drinking vodka. The night was a complete bust. About ten guys came in all night. No one tipped us and my partner got drunk and wild. She made increasingly original attempts to get tips out of the stingy patrons. She started flashing— no tips. Then she started insulting the guys—definitely no tips. She even swung off a beam in the ceiling, like Tarzan—still no tips. At the end of this very dull and fruitless night, the only thing we had to look forward to was the double pay we'd been promised. We lined up for our money. Sal paid us our usual piddling salary. We reminded Sal that he'd promised us double pay. He laughed and said we must have misunderstood him. He had *never* promised any such thing, and we should be glad we'd gotten what we did. I took the money and got my coat, mad as hell but a wiser person for it. Suddenly, *crash!* My wild partner attacked Sal and knocked about two hundred dollars worth of liquor off the bar. I felt better knowing that Sal had been paid for being a lying bastard. The last I heard of Sal, he got some big guy upset, and one night after work the fellow chased him in the back parking lot, caught him, and picked him up and threw him into the garbage dumpster, where he belonged.

One go-go character was called Subway Suzie. She was about forty-five years old and a little unbalanced. She was a bag lady— short, no teeth, and talked to herself a lot. Sometimes you could speak to her and have a normal conversation, but mostly she acted wild. The bars took pity on her, fed her, and let her hang around. She usually caused no problems. Mostly she hung around the jukebox and sang or danced all by herself. No one paid attention to her, and no one made fun of her. We just left her alone. One night, however, she almost caused me to wet myself from laughter. I was dancing on stage, and Subway Suzie was next to the weary bar owner, dancing wildly to the music on the jukebox. Suddenly she started to take her slacks off. Underneath her bag-lady pants was an old-fashioned go-go costume from the 1960s. It had long, white fringe. The bar owner quickly grabbed Suzie and told her to put her slacks back on, but she fought him and tried to whip her sweater off. Suddenly she pulled down her costume as well and shoved her ass into the astonished bar owner's face. When I saw his flailing arms and her bare ass shaking in his face I went into hysterics. I had to drop to the floor of the stage. I doubled over with laughter, tears running down my face.

Another character was a little fat cook named Ida. One of our more shifty patrons was trying to sell stolen cheese wheels. People were buying them, but the bar owner could be fined heavily for aiding the sale of stolen goods, so everything was hush-hush. The cook loved cheese, and the price was right, so she decided to buy one of the cheese wheels. The bar was crowded, so she was extremely cloak and dagger about the purchase. She slipped the money to our crooked patron, and he in turn slipped Ida the hot cheese wheel. The thing was huge, but she slipped the wheel under her sweater so no one would be the wiser. We all knew what was going on, but we couldn't care less. Ida tried to slip out the back door, but she had trouble unlatching it with just one hand. Suddenly, the cheese wheel dropped to the floor and proceeded to roll, nice as you please, down the length of the bar, with people jumping out of its way, until it crashed into the front door and fell over. Ida never served time for buying a hot cheese wheel, but she never lived it down.

In go-go bars there are always cocktail-napkin poets. They fancy themselves in love with the dancers and write deep poetry or little ditties on cocktail napkins for them. I have a scrapbook full of them. Some are quite good. Other patrons enjoy twisting your dollar tip into a ring, a small box, a fan, or sometimes a knot that is almost impossible to unravel. They take great pleasure in watching you try. I never gave them the satisfaction. I waited until I got home.

One skinny dancer everyone called Hot Bones. She was a strange girl who slept in abandoned trains. She would carry two stuffed animals around with her, even up on stage. On her break she talked to no one but the stuffed animals. She called them her children. She was said to have lost custody of her two actual children to her ex-husband and wasn't even allowed visitation rights.

Another dancer we called the Garlic Girl. She was very pretty, but to ward men away from her while on her break she would get a jar of spreadable garlic and rub it on her body. No one would go near her. She didn't make out well in tips, but she did avoid being bothered.

Many go-go customers are gay. Some come in to copy our dance moves, or our makeup techniques. Others come to pick up partners. Once after a set a fellow, about thirty-eight years old and good-looking in a rugged sort of way, motioned to me to sit with him for a drink. He was nice enough and very complimentary. He asked me if I knew a particular young guy who was sitting at the bar. I turned around to see a tall, thin, handsome young man sitting by himself. I didn't know him. He asked me if I would go over to the young man, get to know him, and then introduce them. There would be a twenty-dollar bill in it for me. I told him thanks for the drink, but he'd have to pick up his own guys. While I was dancing my next set, I noticed my host sitting next to the young man. They were drinking together and then left together. One guy explained it to me this way—what better place than a go-go bar to pick up horny guys? If a man gets horny enough watching the dancers but can't have them, maybe he'll settle for another guy.

One strange character was an older man by the name of Robert. He was quiet, very polite, and looked like Mayor Koch. He'd buy the dancers drinks and treat us very well. By the end of the evening, however, he transformed himself into a woman! He then called himself Roberta.

At one point Robert wanted me to be his girlfriend. He wrote down his name and number on a cocktail napkin. I have two napkins from that day—one from the early part of the evening, when he wrote his name down as Robert, and the second from later in the evening, when he wanted me to be his lesbian lover and wrote down his name as Roberta. He'd sit next to macho men in their t-shirts and Michelin caps and paint his fingernails. Once he took off his shoes and started painting his toenails. This was evidently going too far. He was beaten senseless.

A guy named Nick was another strange character. He was about sixty-four and a World War II veteran. He looked like a skinny Boris

Karloff. He liked my act, and as the days passed by and I moved from bar to bar, I saw Nick in my audiences on a regular basis. One day he tipped me, then asked me to join him for a drink. He told me he was a go-go boy and a nude model. He handed me an envelope and told me to take it into the ladies' room and have a good time. My curiosity got the best of me, so I headed for the bathroom. Inside the envelope was a set of eight Polaroid nudes of Nick in various positions. I didn't know whether to laugh, cry, or scream. He looked like a cadaver. I was stunned when I came out. Nick sat there smiling with pride. "Well," he said, "I guess you were really turned on. You were in there a long time." I slowly handed him back the envelope. "No. You keep them and enjoy." He left. Every time I saw Nick after that, he tipped me with a nude photo of himself. Once he walked in all upset with a black eye. "I was at the diner across the street," he explained, "and when I finished I left the waitress a naked photo of me for a tip. She got upset and started screaming, so the owner came out, looked at the photo, and he and another man, I think it was the cook, threw me out of the diner bodily. I didn't even finish my coffee. Can you beat that?"

After a while, Nick asked me to take naked Polaroids of him. He would pay me fifty dollars and pay for the motel room and film. No sex. I only had to photograph him. I passed but I knew other dancers and barmaids who took him up on the offer. Every time he got his monthly pension check it meant new Polaroids and some lucky girl getting to photograph him in the buff.

One day Nick came in all emotional. He asked me if I wanted his huge collection of photograph albums of himself in the raw. He had to get rid of them. His eighty-seven-year-old mother had found them and beaten the shit out of him, so he was looking for a new home for his porno. I passed, of course.

I was constantly on the lookout for new go-go bars to add to the numerous collection of employers I already had. I lived in fear of a bar being closed down. This usually happened if a flasher was caught in the bar or if there was trouble with the fire department or the board of health. This usually meant being closed for forty-five days. I had to constantly scout around for new places just in case. One time I showed up for work to find a note on the door, "Closed due to death in family." No one thought the dancers were important enough to notify. If I had known, I might have been able to book myself at another bar. Instead, I had to go home without the nightly salary I depended on and start to make my gypsy phone calls to other go-go bars. Gypsy phone calls are calls made to go-go bars at random, asking them if their dancers for the night have shown. Sometimes a bar is stuck for a dancer, tells you to come right down, and all is well. Other times you'd fly down to the bar only to find out the girl was just late. "Thanks, but we don't need you after all." On the nights I couldn't find a bar in need, I'd sit all dressed up in full costume, bag packed, next to the phone until about 10:00 P.M. If I didn't get a call by then I was not working that night. The next day I would try for a double shift to make up for the loss.

The bar owners were always trying to get back the money they paid the dancers. Many girls drank heavily, so they were given a tab, and at the end of the night it was deducted from their pay. Sometimes there wasn't much left. The bar owners had another technique, too. They'd sit with the dancers on their breaks and try to get the girls to buy *them* drinks! This happened to me once—but only once. I was on by break when the owner plunked down next to me. He bought me a drink (which, of course, cost him nothing), then asked me why I never bought him a drink. The gall of him! Did he think this was some kind of mutual-admiration society? I told him point blank, "I hate working in these damn bars. I hate the noise and the shit-faced people. I'm working to make money, not to lose it! You have a hell of a nerve asking me to buy you a drink when you own this damn bar and can drink your ass off for free!" Needless to say, that speech didn't make me very popular.

Another bar owner suddenly got very depressed. On my break he asked me to join him for a drink. He had a tale of terrible woe. He was almost fifty, but he had a full head of dyed, jet-black hair and a matching mustache. Nonetheless, recently he had discovered a single white hair on his balls. He wanted to know, "Does this mean I'm growing old?" Was it normal to have white pubic hairs? Could he dye it?

In one bar I worked in, the owner was henpecked by his girlfriend. She was very jealous of all the dancers, so she made things miserable for both him and us. She used to hang around the bar all day and all night to spy on him. She was a homely, out-of-shape, forty-five-year-old woman who wore big, thick glasses and baggy stretch pants. The bar owner was married, and she even got jealous when he went home! The two barmaids were her daughters, so she employed them as spies, too. One of the daughters gave us our bookings. She was a frustrated dancer but never had the nerve to get up and dance herself, so she drank all day and treated the dancers like shit. If we even talked to the bar owner, word got back to his girlfriend and we were chewed out, or, sometimes, let go. One of the hotshot barmaids had herpes. She slept with the whole bar. Then she went to all the guys' homes and said to them, "Surprise, you have herpes." Most men took it in stride, but one guy hauled off and punched her square in the mouth.

One of the go-go bars I worked in had an offer the customers couldn't refuse. On Wednesday nights, for twenty-five dollars, you could get a beer, a blow job, and a hamburger. Now, that sounds like a good deal, until you see the woman who gave the blow jobs. She was about fifty, fat, and had no teeth. Still, men say that women with no teeth give the best blow jobs. I wouldn't know. This particular bar was a kind of brothel on the side. Girls who danced there were expected to spend one night a week "dancing" in the men's room. There were, of course, no facilities to dance in the men's room, only cold, white, pissed-on tile with the jukebox pounding behind the wall. The Wednesday night routine in the "Piss Palace," as it was called, was to dance naked when some asshole came in to take a leak. Then you would come on to him and ask if he wanted a blow job for twenty bucks. In between men coming in and out, you got to sit naked on a cold bar stool and read under a flourescent

light that made you look like shit. I never worked the "Piss Palace."
The boss told me if I wanted to keep my job I had to take my
turn on blow-job night. I quit.

One guy was very nice. He loved all the dancers and was a
perfect gentleman at all times. He was about forty, had never been
married, and was not very handsome. He was funny and witty and
could make anyone laugh, but he was insecure. Every time he came
into a bar he had a different hairstyle. One day he threw me a surprise birthday party. I was supposed to work the lunch shift that
day and I felt bad working on my birthday, but the money I would
lose if I didn't would make me feel worse, so I trudged in. "Surprise!" There were pink and green streamers, balloons, and a crowded
bar. The barmaids carried in a big, rose-covered cake with my name
on it, and champagne flowed all day. This guy had hired a caterer
for the whole affair—all for me. Yes, I danced that day, but not
as usual. I danced *with* the patrons. Even the barmaids were jumping up on the stage and we were taking pictures. The men were
tipping big bills for my birthday. I had fun that day, thanks to a
dear man. Not all the men were pains in the ass, only most of them.

Another nice guy fancied himself in love with me. He was about
thirty-five and still lived at home with his mother, who told him
his father died from the shame of having such a loser for a son.
He was withdrawn and afraid of life. He didn't date. He was afraid
of women, and the most he would do was go to go-go bars and
watch girls. In the heat of summer the guy wore a heavy jacket.
On my breaks, I would sit with him and listen to his problems. I
wanted him to meet a nice girl. Once, when we were in a crowded
bar at a Halloween party, he spotted a pretty girl across the room.
He told me that the week before he'd run into her at another bar.
He'd gotten drunk and run into the ladies' room by mistake. She'd
been combing her long, blonde hair at the mirror, and my friend
puked all over the bathroom right in front of her. He asked me
if I knew her. It just so happens I did know her. She was a bar
hooker and very nice. Would I introduce him to her? Well, I prepped
my friend. I told him to make small talk, then ask her if she'd like

a drink. This is how it went: "Carla, this is my friend Bob. Bob this is Carla." Bob: "I've met you before, remember? I was the guy who puked all over the ladies' room." That was his last chance to get lucky. Back to the drawing board!

Some men claimed a dancer for their own and became very jealous when she got up to dance and other men watched her. Many fights, and even stabbings and shootings, came of this.

One chilly night I had to start work in a new place. Walking into a new bar was always frightening. You never knew what to expect. The place was loud. In one corner guys played pool, in another corner Pac Man. The bar was oval and in the center of it was a small, square platform for a stage. The stage had a skylight over it. During the day that was the dancer's light, raw sunshine. Not only did it make us look terrible, but some of us got sunburned. At night they put on flashing purple lights that made you dizzy. All eyes were on me as I made my way to the stage. A dancer never knows what all the whispering is about when she starts to dance, but it does make you self-conscious. Guys sit together and elbow each other, then cover their mouths and whisper something into their buddies' ears. Grinning, pointing, dirty gestures, and jeers are all part of the job. By the time you come off for your break, you're not sure if the men liked you or hated you.

One young, handsome man tipped me ten dollars during one of my sets, so when he asked me to join him for a drink, I did. He was Irish. We talked and I found him very pleasant. He asked me to join him again on my next break. O.K., he was nice enough! Once again, he tipped me ten dollars while I was dancing. On my break, I did sit with him again, but my job was to sit with a lot of patrons and be friendly—in other words, hustle drinks. So, on my next break, I sat with a very nice black gentleman who bought me a drink. My Irish friend watched me talk to this man from the other side of the bar. Slowly, he turned red in the face, then suddenly came over to confront me. "Why are you sitting with that nigger after I gave you all that money to sit with me?" I explained to him that my boss wanted me to sit with a lot of customers. He called me a tramp and demanded all his tips back. I wasn't sure how much he gave me but thought it was at least thirty dollars. I was mad as hell, but I didn't want to cause a ruckus, so I gave him back thirty dollars. He wanted more. Eventually he settled for what I gave him, but he called me horrible names for the rest of the night. Some of the bar even joined in, but I had to keep dancing. When David came to take me home he knew something was wrong, but I knew better than to tell him. I did finally tell him two hours later, when we were in bed. He went berserk. He dressed quickly and was out the door before I could stop him. He was going to mangle the prick who made my night miserable, but most of the people were gone when he got to the bar. The barmaid told him the guy got into a big fight with a pool player and ended up going to the hospital. He might not have been that lucky if David had caught up with him.

You might be wondering how a dancer can drink with so many men all night and not get drunk. Many dancers do get loaded. I've seen them fall off stages, puke all over themselves right on stage, and even get diarrhea and/or their periods while on stage. But many dancers practice what I call the "bathroom sink cocktail." When a guy buys you a drink, you order something clear, such as white wine, gin, or vodka. Pretend to be sipping it, then excuse yourself and go to the ladies' room. You dump the drink down the drain and refill the glass with water. Never let the guy near your drink. That's how I beat getting drunk and becoming an alcoholic. Besides, it's very hard to dance when you are plastered. Dancing demands full coordination at all times, and I pride myself on being a good dancer. When I drink, I'm on my ear.

In New York City the clubs are strict about dancers hustling drinks for the house. You have to hustle the customers for champagne at thirty-two dollars a glass! Most of the time they actually serve you ginger ale or diluted cherry soda. On your break you have to go to a customer and stand next to him. You're followed by a cocktail waitress who helps you hustle by saying to the customer, "Buy the lady a drink?" If he says yes, you immediately order champagne. When the barmaid plunks down the champagne, you're not supposed to touch it until Charley Brown has been presented with the bill. Usually the men know they are being hustled but don't really mind because they get to be with you. However, some men go crazy (rightfully so). They take it out on the poor dancer, who is only doing as she is told. Sometimes they send the drink back, and sometimes they call the dancer names and throw the drink in her face. Other times they think sex is included in the thirty-two dollars and expect gratification right then and there.

It's not like that in New Jersey. True, the bar would like you to hustle drinks, but no one twists your arm, and drinks are only two dollars. There is far less pressure on the dancer in that respect. Many dancers have come from New York to dance in New Jersey. Dancing in the City wasn't worth the aggravation.

For me, go-go dancing was in truth very grueling work, with the exception of the bookings I had in one bar: "Curt's Lounge." Curt's was not a dim-lit little cocktail lounge. It had a reputation as one of the roughest bars on two continents, and it was. Nonetheless, Curt's was the only bar I loved and felt perfectly safe in. The people were truly good in every sense of the word. The owners, Herman and Bobby, were very fair men. They never made an indecent remark to me. They were very good to me when it came to bookings. Sometimes I worked there almost every day. I remember going to audition at Curt's. Bobby was sitting in the corner of the bar. He was a very handsome man who resembled a young Clark Gable. He took one look at me in my green sequined costume and said, "Skip the audition. You're hired." I was part of the Curt's family from then on.

It was actually fun to dance there. No one made rude remarks to the dancers in Curt's. The management always took the dancer's side and the troublemaker was out on his ear. The barmaids never told you that you had to hustle champagne. In fact, you didn't have to hustle drinks at Curt's at all. If all you wanted to drink was club soda, well, that was O.K. In many go-go bars, if you buy the dancer a soda, you get charged two dollars, the same as an alcoholic beverage. Not in Curt's—soda was fifty cents, plain and simple. Curt's was the only bar that didn't expect the dancers to flash, and the patrons didn't want it anyway. It was a family bar. Lots of times the men brought their wives, and the owners wanted you to keep your act clean. Curt's had a softball team. Every Saturday there was a game. All the players wore great-looking navy blue and light blue jerseys with "Curt's" printed on them. At the time, I was doing some modeling and I thought it would be nice if I posed in one of those baseball jerseys and made a poster for the bar. Herman liked the idea, so I was lent a jersey, number twenty-nine. I made up the poster and gave it to Curt's in appreciation for all they had done for me. The poster was proudly displayed over the cash register. One day, to my amazement, Bobby and Herman presented me with my very own Curt's jersey, with my name on the back.

Getting to work and back wasn't always easy, especially in the snow. One evening there was a storm warning for the next day. We were supposed to get eight to ten inches of snow, but in the morning it looked clear, albeit very cold. I had to dance at a go-go bar from 12:00 noon to 7:00 P.M. I didn't think I should call in just because of the alleged snow. I couldn't afford to lose the day's pay, and what if it didn't snow? So I was off to work. I was the first dancer on, meaning I had to dance from noon until 12:20 P.M., the first set. At lunchtime the bar was full. While I was dancing I noticed that the men walking in seemed to have white hair—it had started snowing, just as predicted! On my break I peeked outside to see what was going on. Sure enough, the ground was covered in snow, which was coming down in a fine powder. I decided to wait it out. As the afternoon progressed, things got progressively worse. The men weren't going back to work. It was standing-room-only as people packed into the bar for shelter. Business, needless to say, was great.

I was worried about our car. It was not in very good shape. When it was time to quit I noticed David wasn't waiting in the bar as he usually did. I kept on my costume of purple sequins and jumped straight into my long, black pantsuit. I bundled up and left to wait outside for David. I never felt so alone. The roads had no cars on them. All I could see was the blizzard and a dark dismal street. I stood there with snowflakes melting my makeup and saturating my hair. I got too cold. I went back inside to use the ladies' room but thought better of it when I saw what was going on. The other dancer had decided to stay and make extra money. She was beyond flashing— she was half naked and the men were in a frenzy. She was the only female in a room full of horny, snowbound men. I got my ass pinched and decided to take my chances with the snow. Home was only fifteen minutes away. After half an hour I got worried. Where was David? After about forty-five minutes, I saw headlights in the distance. Sure enough, it was David. I was never so happy to see him. Now I'd be warm and cozy, and get to see my kids. Wrong! It took us two and a half hours to get home. Driving was impossible. Cars were stuck all over the place. The heat didn't work in our car, and the windshield wipers froze up. David couldn't see a thing, so he had to drive with one hand, scraping ice off the windshield with the other. We crawled along the road. On several occasions the entire car spun around in a circle, completely out of control. We got stuck. Our wheels kept spinning. A guy in a jeep with a plow on the front drove up next to us and said, "It looks like you people need help. It'll cost you a hundred dollars." David told him to go sleep with himself. The guy left and we tried to get out ourselves. I ran the motor while David went out and pushed. It was no use. Then a group of little boys, about ten and twelve years old, ran up and offered to get us out for five dollars. We hired them. The bunch of them literally dug us out with their mittened hands. When they got us out, their leader came to the window, runny nose, reddened cheeks, and soaked, and held out his hand. We handed him a twenty. It was well worth it. As we drew nearer to home our car started to stall. We got out and walked. I had no boots, only silver high heels—open-toed. The snow was up to our knees. We had to plow through deep snowdrifts while being blinded by freezing sleet. Miraculously, I didn't catch a cold. I never danced under the threat of a storm warning again.

My health was suffering from double shifts. My hearing was going from being exposed to loud pounding music all the time. I found myself not being able to hear the television and yelling in restaurants or movies. My feet were a mass of blisters and calluses. Toenail polish never stayed on. I wore out a pair of expensive silver high heels every week. I had a deal with the shoe store to keep me stocked in this particular style shoe. My lungs, throat, and eyes burned from inhaling smoke. Most stages were up close to the ceiling, which was where the cigarette smoke rose. Naturally, I also had to inhale deeply from all the exertion. In some places the air was filled with pot, which was much worse.

One night I was booked at a new bar. It had a bad reputation, but I didn't find this out until I'd already started dancing. I might have known something was wrong when I found out I would be the only dancer that night. The bar was packed with rowdy foreigners wearing black leather jackets and cleaning guns and knives at the bar. I went over very big, but I was very tense. The men looked at me like they wanted to eat me alive. On my break they were grabbing my ass and pulling me over to talk to them. One guy pulled me onto his lap and I couldn't get up. There was no bouncer. I later learned they couldn't keep one because there were so many fights. They followed me to the dressing room. I had to lock myself in—something I had never had to do in any of the bars I had danced in before. I really wasn't sure I was going to get out of there in one piece. On one of my breaks I was asked to join a young man at the bar for a drink. He was from Ireland. He'd been in America for just two weeks. He was polite, very nice, and very handsome. He was also new to the bar. We were the only two Irish people in the whole place. Everybody—believe it or not—was Albanian. As this fellow talked to me, I noticed we were being watched by the others. He noticed it, too, and said to me, "Should there be any trouble, hide behind the bar, O.K.?" I said I would, "But what do you mean by trouble?" He said, in his thick Irish brogue, "Never mind. Just do what I say." Now I was really scared. I got up behind the bar and started dancing. My Irish friend got up to go to the men's room, but he was attacked by four men in black leather jackets. He was a hell of a fighter and was beating the daylights out of the four of them, but three more jumped in and held his arms while the other four beat him to a pulp. They punched him repeatedly in the stomach, slammed his head into a wall, tore his shirt completely off, and punched his front teeth out. Finally they stabbed him in the stomach.

The bar owner was drunk, but he went to his safe, took out a gun, and started waving it around in the air. I was petrified! I belatedly did as the Irishman told me and hid under the bar. The last I saw of my Irish friend, he was being dragged out the door. He was half-conscious, his once-handsome face was a bloody pulp, and his naked stomach was gushing black blood. They threw him into the snow. David was due to pick me up in ten minutes, and I kept thinking, "Please don't let him walk into a gunfight." I dressed quickly. By the time I came out, David was there, looking pretty rough himself. He has an uncanny way of knowing when something is wrong. He saw some Albanians blocking my way, pushed through them with his meanest face, then elbowed the both of us through the crowd of leather jackets. Outside the snow was covered in dark blood and my Irishman was gone.

One night I was wearing a bra all covered in gold coins, like a belly dancer's top. On my break I was stopped by two well-dressed young men. I had never seen such crisp black suits and immaculate black overcoats. One said to the other, "I bet she has two hundred gold coins on her bra." The other said, "I'll bet you a hundred dollars she has three hundred coins on her bra." They asked me how many coins were on the bra. "Do you think I don't have better things to do than count the coins on my bra?" He replied, "I'll give you a dollar to count them." I told him that for that money the number of coins would have to remain a mystery. In reality, curiosity had driven me to count the coins soon after I bought the bra. There were exactly 272.

Later I found out that the two big spenders were wealthy funeral directors. They didn't tell anyone what they did for a living because many people, particularly women, would get turned off. I told one of them that I'd heard that some undertakers kept dead cats in shoe boxes under their beds as children. He responded, "What's wrong with that?" One dancer, unaware of their profession, told them, "My fantasy is making love in a casket." That was all she had to say. I heard they fulfilled her every fantasy, and then some!

One patron asked to buy me a drink and told me he was a wealthy Arab sheik. He said he was "in love" with me and wanted to add me to his harem. It was very flattering, but I told him, "No, thank you." I went back on stage to dance and he watched me closely. Then he watched the men watching me. At one point, when I was kidding around with one of the regulars, I noticed him tapping his fingers on the bar impatiently. On my next break, he bought me another drink, then squeezed my hand really hard, gritted his teeth together, and said, "You enjoy flaunting your flesh? I can't stand to see other men's eyes upon you. I would like to strike them blind!" I was getting a little frightened of the sheik, so I left him and went to the jukebox to select my songs. The place was crowded. The music was blaring, and people were crammed together dancing, talking loudly, and fighting. There was a big pool game. The barmaids were working double time. Suddenly I felt the sheik behind me. He was leaning over my shoulder and pressing something hard into my back. He whispered in an angry voice with breath that smelled like booze, "If you don't come with me, I'll kill you right here, and no man will have that which is mine!" I was panic-stricken but somehow remained level-headed. I stared at the brightly lit song titles on the jukebox while my mind raced for an answer. I told him, "I get off at 2:00 A.M. Let me finish the night's work here, then I'll go with you."

I told him, "Why don't you leave now, because I know it upsets you watching me dance in front of all these men. But come back at 2:00 A.M. Then I'll be all yours, and yours only." The sheik was beside himself with joy. He kissed my neck, then squeezed me and said, "I'm just leaving until two o'clock, my love." As he left, I looked at the clock. It was twenty to nine. I got off in fifteen minutes. I danced while trembling all over. My knees were weak and banging together. I told David what happened, and he told me I had danced my last dance as a go-go girl. I was free!

Pop had been living with us for more than two years. Soon after he moved in he suffered a very mild heart attack. The doctors immediately put Pop on a diet and told him there could be no more drinking or smoking. My father wanted me to quit dancing and take care of him, but that was impossible at the time. He just had to settle for David taking care of him. He was rough on David. My father had to be watched at all times. David had to be sure Pop took his medication every day and keep him from sneaking a smoke in his room or going to the bar downstairs for a quick shot of whiskey.

While I had been dancing, Pop had been feeling like I was neglecting him. He wanted me home taking care of his every whim and need. He thought of his stomach, and filling it, twenty-four hours a day. He wasn't happy with the way David cooked, and plus David had a queer habit of serving a fresh salad with every meal. I was supposed to be home like a real wife and mother. What he didn't understand somehow was that I was supporting him, and if I stayed home he wouldn't eat. I sat across the table from him one night, with dark circles under my eyes and aching, bleeding feet. I'd just finished a double shift. I'd had to take my shoes off while walking up the back steps because blood ran down my heels with every step. He looked me in the eye and said in his nastiest tone, "There's no liverwurst in the icebox. Some daughter you are!" Then he stormed off to his room. When he slammed his door, that was the ball game. I flew up in a rage, followed him, and threw open his door. There he sat, sipping wine and watching television. I picked up the bottle of wine and flung it against the wall. Then, I ranked him out for being a selfish bastard. I felt bad afterwards, but I was hardly in control anymore. After being a go-go dancer, you are always on the defensive. You develop a vocabulary worthy of the quarterdeck of a battleship.

After I quit dancing, I got to sleep until noon every day. I was so happy to be home for good. David would not let me do any work at all, not even a dish. He waited on me hand and foot. Despite this treatment, my health took a turn for the worse. My body started to lock up on me from not dancing anymore. All my muscles got stiff and painfully sore. I could hardly walk. My back felt like it was broken. We made plans to visit David's parents down in Alabama for Christmas. Then we would drive to Disney World. I invited Pop to come down South with us. I thought he would love Disney World. We'd have a great Christmas. For some reason he didn't want to go. He decided to lay a guilt trip on me instead. "You go ahead, leave me alone on Christmas, it's O.K." I didn't care. Nothing was going to stand in my way. For all the time I danced my butt off, I got nothing for myself; this was for me. If Pop wanted to make a martyr out of himself, that was his business. He was more than welcome to come along.

I laid in food supplies for my father and a case of his favorite wine. I baked him two cakes and left him his Christmas presents. He was not satisfied. He wanted pickle spears, Vlasic pickle spears. After some annoying searching I found the damn pickle spears, Vlasic. My father's only responsibility while we were gone was to feed my eleven cats. I left him all the cat food he would need. He only had to scoop it out.

We were off. We started early on a sunny morning—driving down South would be an exciting adventure. Along the way, we stopped at nice restaurants, took pictures, and bought souvenirs. Breakfast down South is excellent. All meals are served with homemade biscuits. I wasn't worried about my weight. I'd lost a lot of weight dancing, too much weight. I could stand a few pounds, and I was going to have fun putting them on.

We finally got to David's family home in Alabama. We shared a great Christmas. New Year's Eve was a family affair. I got a little tipsy on champagne, but I owed myself a good time. Besides, the alcohol helped relieve the continuing pain in my legs and back.

It was time to start packing up for Florida. Every day we were gone I called my father to say hello and make sure he was alright.

After about a week something strange began to take place. Pop started reporting that some of my cats had died. What was wrong? The cats were fine when we left.

We left David's parents for Florida. The state was beautiful. It was a thrill seeing palm trees. Our first stop was going to be Busch Gardens. I had been there seven years before, but I couldn't get enough of the place, and, of course, David and the kids had never seen it, so I was keen on showing them around. I got the usual brass knick-knacks, doodads, and souvenirs to bring home. Being a belly dancer, I love Busch Gardens' Moroccan marketplace atmosphere and the Middle Eastern music. We treated the kids to elephant rides and twisted crullers with fresh orange juice. There was a wonderful belly-dance show, and the kids particularly liked the snake dancer. We spent a full day there, then went to dinner. Next day was Disney World.

I slept well that night. I was so happy, I felt reborn. The morning came fast. I was up before anyone, did my makeup, and waited for the others to wake. It was a clear, sunny, wonderful day. Palm trees swayed lazily in the cool breeze, and little dew drops glistened like diamonds on the plant leaves. We finally got to our destination. When I first saw Disney Castle, my eyes started to water. The day was perfect, and we practically had the whole place to ourselves. I wore a pair of Mickey Mouse ears and so did David and Jack. Juliet wore a Goofy hat. The next day found us in the Epcot Center, a real adventure. The restaurants there were beautiful. We ate in a Mexican Village there.

Going home was sad. We were all silent in our own thoughts. No one wanted to go, but it was time to get back to real life. David was going to take over as the sole supporter of the family, and I was going to stay home and take care of Pop and the kids. It was a long drive home, and after being away so long the New York skyline was a welcome sight. We were all hungry, so we decided to get a couple pizzas and champagne for a quick meal when we got home.

We got in around 10:00 P.M. Pop hadn't expected us until the following day, so he was caught by surprise. He was sitting at the table, drinking whiskey, loaded to the gills. In the middle of the table was a pile of napkins, which he'd just set on fire, slowly burning out. The house looked like a bomb had hit it. And there was a bad smell coming from somewhere. What was it? Ashtrays overflowed. Cigarette butts had been put out on the kitchen floor. Dishes were piled high in the sink, soaking in slimy water. Grease covered my stove and the floor. Pork chop bones and the plastic containers they had come in were scattered all over the floor. Things were spilled all over the inside of the refrigerator and it stank.

The worst was yet to come. In the dish rack lay one of my cats, its mouth wide open, dried blood oozing from its ears and nose. Alongside the stove was an outline of dried blood in the form of a cat. Where was the cat? I went to the room Pop shared with my son and found blood-stained sheets on my son's bed. Under it lay another cat, stiff with blood coming from its eyes, ears, and nose. Another cat lay behind the couch, the same as the others. I noticed a broken glass on the floor behind the couch. Looking up I saw a dried stream of wine running down the wall. I found two cats barely alive, emaciated and very weak. My favorite cat, Mr. Blue, a large, blue alley cat, attacked me when I tried to hug him. This was totally out of his character. He was so tense you couldn't get near him.

I demanded to know just what the hell happened, but my father was incoherent. He said he didn't know what had happened to the cats. Anyway, if I loved those cats so much, then why did I leave them on Christmas? I was enraged, but I didn't want to take it out on Pop. He looked seriously ill. The house was so filthy we couldn't sit down. David went to an all-night supermarket and loaded up on cleaning utensils and cleaners. We cleaned dry blood and filth until 8:00 in the morning. Just after midnight Pop complained of pains in his chest and demanded to be rushed to the hospital. He refused to go by ambulance. Instead, he insisted I call my brother and have him drive him to the hospital.

Jack was an ambulance driver and a police officer. He'd just got done working sixteen hours and was dead tired, but he got dressed and came over. He looked exhausted. Pop had been running him into the ground the whole time I'd been gone. Before they left for the hospital, Pop insisted I find him his "sexy" hat. With his dry wit my brother gave him Juliet's Goofy hat. Pop had to stay in the hospital overnight. When he came home he was shaky. He was put on a strict diet, given heart pills, and told he could do absolutely no drinking!

David started work, and once again I was in charge of the house. I had to make sure Pop took his medication and ate properly. He was grumpy, but I was in no mood for his shenanigans. Basically, he did what he was told.

Saturday came. It was a nice day. David and I planned a quiet day together. I'd brought two big bags of pecans all the way from Georgia to make a pecan pie, my first. Pop acted strange all day. He was nervous and shaky. That's not unusual when an alcoholic stops drinking. He was breathing heavily. He spent all day watching television in his room. David and I were cracking nuts for the pie, listening to Pop's heavy breathing. That wasn't too unusual either. Pop was very heavy and often had labored breathing.

All of a sudden Pop's room fell silent. David went to check on him. Pop seemed to be sleeping, but he looked strange. His tongue was hanging out. He felt cold. We shook him, but he didn't move. We realized he was dead.

I called my brother, who was working as a police officer that day. We had to wait for the medical examiner to come and pronounce Pop dead. But this was a Saturday, and no medical examiner was to be found. Pop lay dead in his bed for about five hours before he was finally pronounced dead. It took six men to carry him down the stairs. He was taken out in a body bag, which resembled a large garbage bag to me. That was the end of "Westy," a real character.

In the wake of Pop's death, feline leukemia swept the house. The cats who had survived Pop's neglect were now struck with this dreaded disease. It cost David a small fortune in veterinarian bills. David wasn't making a fortune. No matter what he made, I still had made more money go-go dancing, so we had to scrimp a lot. Eventually we lost all of our cats except Mr. Blue, who is still with me today. Pop's death, followed by weeks and weeks of regular loss of our pets, left me numb. Then David's mom got sick. She was diagnosed as having lung cancer. She went fast, dying like a dog, like my mom, and leaving David's father bitter and cold. Things were getting bad. Our car started going. David had to pour money into it every week, and we couldn't afford it.

I took some modeling jobs to help out, but I couldn't get that many. I thought I could pose for men's magazines because I had a good figure. But most of the times I went to a photographer for an evaluation I got the brush off. "You're too short." "You're too fat. Lose ten pounds." "You're too old." "You're not pretty enough to be a model." "Maybe you can get photographed holding a can of Comet." "How come your nose isn't in the middle of your face?"

Of all the insults hurled at me, the nose cracks bothered me the most. I hated my nose. It had been broken three times, and it did ruin my face. I grew very depressed. More than anything I wanted a nose job, but I knew we could never afford one. David would drive me to photographers' studios, just to pick me up in tears. Once I was told, "You're homely. I don't want to waste film on you."

As a child I had always been called homely. When I was six my girlfriend and I put on a mock Miss America Pageant. Our mothers were supposed to be the judges. My mother voted for my girlfriend. Then I heard her say to another mother, "Your Susan is beautiful, but mine is so plain and mousy." My father used to tell me the same, to the tune of "There's No Place Like Home": "Be it ever so homely, there's no face like your own."

As a small child I had large buckteeth and freckles all over. My hair was dull brown and cut in a squared-off, Buster Brown style. As a teenager, the freckles turned into pimples and ugly blackheads. I remember always wondering what it would be like to be pretty. More than anything I wanted a pretty face. I didn't care about a good body, I would settle for just a pretty face. I used to fantasize about people remarking on my beauty. It wasn't in the cards. I was Pimple Face, Bucky Beaver, Dog Face. I was told I could stop a clock just by looking at it. It got so bad that I didn't come out to sit on the front porch until it was dark. I was afraid of offending someone with my face.

David knew all too well how I viewed myself, so one day he surprised me with a visit to a plastic surgeon. The doctor looked at my nose and told me it would be a simple matter to straighten it. But the work would be costly. I left feeling worse. Now I knew it *could* be fixed but definitely never *would* be. I remember recalling the antiseptic smell of the doctor's office and the thought that within its walls was the solution to one of my deepest insecurities. That doctor, his hands, could change the whole way I felt about myself. I went home and cried my eyes out. David was sick. He couldn't stand seeing me so unhappy. He wanted to give me everything, but he couldn't afford it. Never had I been so loved. David worked in New York City for a collection agency. It wasn't the greatest job, but at a time when jobs were so scarce, it was a wonderful thing for us. David was determined to get my nose fixed, so he went out and got a higher-paying job—as a garbage collector!—and added on a night job as a security guard. I know how degrading it must have been for a man with college degrees to work these menial jobs.

Every morning he'd rise at about 3:00 A.M., dress in a dirty pair of jeans, work gloves, and a hooded jogging sweatshirt, and go out and hang on the back of filthy, smelly garbage trucks. I always knew when he collected at the fish markets. When he came home, you could smell rotted fish a mile away. He wore out a pair of work gloves every other day. Twice he sprained his wrists from lifting the garbage cans the wrong way. Once he twisted his ankle jumping off the trucks, and twice he was almost killed by passing cars. One day there were police and detectives all over the landfill he dumped at, poking through the mounds of garbage. They were looking for the body of a young girl. They eventually found her there. David's new circumstances left him very depressed, but he forged on. David had once been a first lieutenant in the Army, and one day, at a nice home in a nice neighborhood, he ran into one of the men he had commanded. The young fellow looked at David as if he knew him, but David quickly emptied the guy's garbage before he could figure out who he was and then took off.

We saved enough money so that I could be scheduled for surgery. I was told it was going to hurt, but I didn't care. I'd wanted it for so long. We had almost all the money we needed. We were short about four hundred dollars. We had only one person to turn to for help—my Uncle Dick. At my father's funeral my very rich uncle had insisted to me, should I ever need help in any way, should I ever need money, not to hesitate to call him. "Please!" So I called and asked for a loan of four hundred dollars. I promised to pay it back in three weeks. Uncle Dick said just one thing, "Will Monday be soon enough?" Since it was Saturday, Monday was fine. I was supposed to call him Sunday night to confirm things. Things couldn't be better. By Wednesday I would have a new nose. Sunday night I called Uncle Dick. This is exactly what he said: "Did you call me Saturday and ask to borrow some money?" I said yes, to which he replied, "Isn't that funny? You must have gotten me when I was half asleep. I can't lend you any money. I don't have it to give. But I'll take your problem to the Lord. God bless."

As it turned out, I didn't need the two-faced bastard. Somehow David squared it away with the doctor, and Wednesday found me in an ear, nose, and throat infirmary in New York City.

The day consisted of tests and getting my old schnozz photographed. That night I remember looking out my window at the bright city lights and thinking, "Someday I'll be famous here." I was too keyed up to sleep, so the nurses gave me a sedative. The next morning I was up early. I was nervous and a little scared. In the immortal words of some well-meaning friends, this wasn't no haircut, it wouldn't grow back. The nurses gave me a shot in the can, a muscle relaxant. I kept waiting to fall asleep, but I didn't. I was wheeled down to the operating room wide awake! "Oh, shit!" When I saw my doctor I reminded him that I was still awake. "When will I be knocked out?" He said I would remain awake throughout the operation. I could watch. Wouldn't that be fun? Finally I realized my doctor was a practical joker. He was only kidding. But then I was wheeled into the operating room, still quite conscious. I suddenly realized he wasn't kidding at all.

The first thing he did was shine a huge light in my face. I was almost blinded. Doc looked like a shadow, and so did his assistants. Next, he bent my abused nose back and forth, then cleaned it with alcohol and commenced to shoot my nose up with long needles. I must admit, by the time he pulled the needles out, my entire face was numb. As the operation proceeded, I felt no pain, but I could hear cracking sounds as Doc broke my nose. I could hear him sawing on my nose bone, too. But I felt nothing, honestly, and Doc was all done before I knew it.

There it was in the mirror, my new nose. I stood looking at this swollen-feeling thing in the middle of my face that was bandaged up like the Mummy. There was no way to tell if it was a good job or a bad job. It was now a waiting game—the bandages would come off in a week. In the meantime, I was told, "Don't sneeze!" Now, I had no intention of sneezing, until I was restricted from it. All of a sudden I just had to sneeze. Automatically, a light went on in my head blinking, "Sneeze, sneeze, sneeze." Fortunately Doc gave me lessons on how to sneeze through my mouth. Where would we be without modern medicine? All week I felt like the Invisible Man. Maybe when they took off the bandages, my nose would be gone. Or maybe it would look ten times worse—a giant gash in my face. Maybe they took off too much, and I would look like the Phantom of the Opera.

The day came. I was nervous. I didn't want to see it just as much as I did. Never look to a doctor's face for answers. They've been trained in medical school not to give away any information via facial expression. I could have looked like a gorilla, but Doc was deadpan as he snipped the bandages away. I anxiously asked him, "How did it turn out?" He answered by sticking a hand mirror in my hands. "You tell me." I was afraid to look, but I did. I was thrilled beyond belief. My nose was tiny and pointed, just like I had always wanted. I used to envy girls with noses like that. "Wow!" Now I looked great.

My modeling started picking up, but David was still running himself into the ground with his two jobs. I wanted to change my appearance altogether to really get things going with my modeling. But what should I do? One day I realized that enough was enough. David was getting ready for work on the garbage trucks. He looked like a bum. It was freezing cold out, and all he had to wear was a hooded sweatshirt. He had no gloves or scarf. When I saw him pin a sweat sock around his neck to keep out the cold, I started crying. That night I told him I was going back to work. I didn't want to go back to go-go dancing, but I had to do something. David didn't want me to work again, but he knew that when I made up my mind there was no stopping me. I was going to New York City to find work.

Burlesque

Finding work as a stripper would be easy because I had experience, confidence, and a gimmick. With my bag of clothes slung over my shoulder, I approached the Harmony Burlesque. I looked at the marquee, read the headliners' names, gazed at the strippers' photos in the display, and went in.

More winding stairs! When I reached the top I saw beautiful, larger-than-life photos of strippers from the past. A very nice young woman named Monique greeted me. Monique was a sharp businesswoman. She was part owner and ran the entire theater. I told her I was interested in a job stripping. She asked me if I had any experience. I said yes. I was told to have a seat in the lobby until the main owner, Bob, came out of his office.

The lobby had two quite comfortable vinyl couches, red walls, display cases showing the current dancers, a soda machine, and restrooms. It was a couple of steps up to get into the actual theater. There was a reddish glow coming from the doorway. I heard music, and men began filing in. They glanced down at me sitting on the vinyl couch with my bag on my lap. The soda machine had a big, makeshift sign taped to it: "Now we have Cherry Coke." A few strippers came up the steps, bags over their shoulders. They looked at me, then sat on the other couch. I heard them talking. They were working later that day.

The music stopped, there was a round of applause, and the men starting streaming out. They all looked at me. In a few minutes a stripper in a flowered bathrobe came out. She was sweating, her hair was pinned up, and she was wiping her neck with a scarf. She came over to the soda machine and got herself a Cherry Coke. She looked down at me, then she plunked herself down next to me. I started what I thought was a friendly conversation. "Hot in there?" She looked at me, then got up and went back inside the theater. I remembered how unfriendly everybody had been when I started at my old place. Here we go again!

The door to the office opened and out came a very handsome man, about fifty, I thought. He looked like a combination of William Holden and a young George Raft. He was well dressed in a sports jacket and neat slacks, hands shoved deep in his pockets—his trademark, as it turned out.

Bob took one look at me and said, "You're hired. If you have your costumes you can start today." It was burlesque, round two. Naturally, in the beginning I had to eat dirt from all the other dancers. I didn't have to start as a fill-in stripper, at least. I was made a gold star stripper right from the start. I was strong now. My act was superior, and I not only demanded respect from the audience, I got it.

In my estimation, the Harmony was the last of the real burlesque theaters in Times Square. It was famous for its beautiful girl revues, and it was clean—no raunch whatsoever. In time the girls came to like me. Some even tried to emulate my act. One of my trademarks was to wear a long string of pearls down my back. This caught on like wildfire. The next thing I knew, everybody was wearing pearls backwards.

Harmony was one big family. We all stuck together like sisters. We could trust each other, which, after go-go dancing, I found hard to believe. Nevertheless, it was true. Bob was our father figure. I found out he was not fifty, despite his devilishly handsome features. He was seventy! Bob had sung with the big bands of the 1940s. He grew up in Hoboken, New Jersey. Frank Sinatra was a childhood pal. In between strip acts, the theater would plug Bob's songs, like "I'll Never Smile Again" and "I'll Be Seeing You." He sounded great! Sometimes, if we were lucky, Bob would sing us a song out in the lobby, hands shoved deeply into his pants pockets. He had an incredibly strong voice. We couldn't get enough. Bob particularly liked me because I knew a lot of songs from the 1940s. Sometimes on my break I'd go out in the lobby and we'd sing together. Needless to say, Bob's voice had to carry me. I'm no singer, but I know the words.

The man was also a true gentleman. Never did he say one out-of-the-way thing to me or any of the other dancers. He treated all of us with respect and understanding. Bob was literally surrounded with beautiful girls who all loved him. If any of us were feeling low because of our period—and there was always at least one of us with our period—Bob would say, "O.K. Go home, get rest. I'll work around it."

He never yelled at us, which is not to say that he didn't have a temper or that he was a pushover. Bob had a wild temper when he was mad, but he was never mad at us. His anger was usually directed at an unruly customer, say, a wiseass heckling the dancers. Once we saw Bob throw a smartass right down the stairs. He was definitely no pushover.

Bob loved my old-time burlesque act so much so he gave me the title, the "Queen of Burlesque." It stuck. From then on, I was introduced as the "Queen of Burlesque," and men came to see my act from all over—not just from New York. There was a lawyer all the way from Virginia who came in to see my act. He'd heard I was a good performer from a close friend, so he came in to see for himself. He was very pleased, and I frequently found him sitting in the audience. Talk about commuting! I once had an army general come in to see my act. He brought some friends along with him, a colonel and a major. They treated me to dinner between shows.

There were several funny characters who came to see my show. One was a slippery-looking guy called "Teddie the Pervert." Teddie wasn't really a pervert, although he can safely claim he has been thrown out of every strip theater in New York City. Teddie loved to slap girls on the bare bottom. "Whack!" No touching was allowed in these places, so poor Teddie got the heave-ho daily, ass over neck down the long stairways of burlesque theaters. All the girls and management came to know him. He was really a likable guy. You just had to know how to take him.

I started out in a love-hate relationship with Teddie. I remember coming out on stage one day to find Teddie in the front row with his hat on his lap, doing something he shouldn't have been doing. I kept my eye on him all through my act. When it was over, I went backstage to my dressing room, put on my robe, and took a rolled-up newspaper with me out into the audience. It was intermission, and a lot of guys were getting up to stretch their legs. I went into one of the rows, climbed over a couple seats and managed to get directly behind oblivious Teddie, who was still doing naughty things. Suddenly I cracked him on the head with the rolled-up newspaper. He was flabbergasted. Then I read him the riot act. He got so nervous he dropped his hat. After that Teddie wasn't too keen on me, but eventually we became civil to each other.

There was also a delightful gentleman called "Frenchy." He was an older man with a beard and sparkling eyes. Frenchy was from France alright. He had a thick French accent. Every time we saw him, he was wearing a different hat. His favorite was a ten-gallon hat. We loved Frenchy because he made a habit of leading the men into loud applause. Frenchy loved strippers. He was very generous with tips. We could have a lot of fun with him. We would steal his hat from him. He always went along with our teasing. We always joked that he was a fur trapper, because he looked like one.

Another regular was a big, heavy guy named Zach. This fellow always brought a shopping bag full of sandwiches, sodas, potato salad, chips, cookies, and chocolate candy, not to mention hundreds of dollars in crisp, brand-new dollar bills. He would take his seat in the front row, whip out a sandwich, and start his party. When he came, Zach was there for the whole day. He'd tip us all, generously, and keep tipping us the whole day. He wouldn't leave until all his money—seven hundred dollars was the usual amount—was completely gone.

In between shows, the tech man would play music. Now, during the day, if Bob ran the music, we'd get his songs and songs by Frank Sinatra. But come six o'clock in the evening there would be a changing of the guard. Ralph would come in. Ralph played nothing but Connie Francis tapes. He loved her. Back in the dressing rooms, if we heard Connie singing "Frankie My Love," we knew Ralph was in. One night I sat in the audience between shows discussing the day's events with a regular customer. Ralph was blasting us with Connie Francis. The customer started to overdose on her songs. Suddenly he said to me, dead serious, nodding in Ralph's direction, "You know, they never did catch the man who raped Connie Francis."

As the Queen of Burlesque, I was given the best dressing room— it had a glitzy star on the door. The room was spacious and quite comfortable and all mine. I couldn't help thinking how far I had come from dressing in the hallway and hanging my clothes on doorknobs. My customers looked forward to my shows, so I felt responsible for giving my best performance each time. Sometimes, however, I didn't feel quite up to it. Once I had a fever of 102° and an infected throat. I had chills all day and by night it started getting worse. I should have been home in bed, but to leave on such short notice would not have been right, so I went on. My audience was never the wiser, but when I bent over to pick up my costumes after the performance, the room started spinning. Luckily, there was a mirrored post for me to lean on to keep from falling. One of the regulars advised me to gargle with fresh lemon juice, salt, and warm water. He said it would kill the infection in my throat. I was desperate, doubtful but desperate. But where would I get fresh lemons so late at night? While I bundled up for the cold trek down to the Port Authority bus terminal, the guy with the advice about the lemons ran out and found me some. That was awfully thoughtful of him. The night air was brutal. I was burning with fever as I forged on to the terminal. On the bus, I thought I was going to die, and then all my lemons would go rolling down the aisle. I didn't die. When I got home, I did as I was told, made my lemon drink, proceeded to gargle with it, and then went straight to bed. The next morning I felt like a million dollars. My fever broke and my throat wasn't sore anymore—it was a miracle.

I love music. I'm always humming a tune, or blasting the stereo, or listening to the radio. I really can't say that I have a favorite kind of music. I love 1950s and 1960s music. In fact, I'm somewhat of an expert on the "do-wop" bands. I also love both country western music and cowboy music, which are very different. I listen to Irish music and understand every word the singers sing. There is nothing like bagpipes to get my blood pumping. Then there're my belly-dance albums. I'm even on the cover of one of them, *The Sound of Greece.* These songs are mainly Greek, Turkish, Lebanese, and Egyptian. I can't read the blurbs on the covers of these records, and the singers could be swearing like hell when they sing, for all I know. Whatever they're doing, it sounds great to me.

I had my son make me up a heavy metal tape one day. I exercise to it and breeze through my housework blasting Guns and Roses, Iron Maiden, Metallica, Skid Row, and Aerosmith. Metal songs are very invigorating, to say the absolute least. No, I don't feel like committing suicide or murdering my family while listening to this kind of music. I cannot stand opera in any form, folk songs, or rap.

I was doing well in burlesque, but the fact was that I remained a little green in the world of Times Square, a world unto its own. One day I was approached by an older dancer, who asked me if I was interested in dancing at a convention. There would be a number of dancers, including us. She was the star. We would be dancing for four hundred men at a plush hotel in New York City. There was a hundred dollars in it for me. Being new to stripping and feeling a bit cocky with my newfound fame, I said yes. I knew I could handle any situation.

On the appointed night, all the dancers working the convention were dismissed from the burlesque theater. David and I showed up early, to get the feel of the audience. We peeked into the huge hall to see the audience. Hundreds of conventioners were drinking their asses off. Down the middle of the crowd ran a long, long runway, which turned out to be just a lot of tables pushed together and covered in white tablecloths! There was a band, but it was barely audible over all the loud talking and laughter. The stage lighting was far from the soft, red and amber lights of the theater. They were hard white house lights, burning brightly through a thick haze of smoke. "Oh, boy."

I was ushered into our dressing room. Actually, it was a big ladies' lounge with a lot of mirrors surrounded by white makeup bulbs. The carpet was thick red plush. Some of the other dancers were there already, and they were drinking heavily. The star was there, and she was drinking, too.

The star told me that two girls would be on stage at one time, one at one end, another to dance with at the other end. We would finish the show with the most important act of all—"the finale."

What was the finale? The "Star" smiled and said, "You'll see. Just be sure you're there." I tried asking some of the other dancers what the finale was like, but they just shook their heads and said to wait and see. While applying my makeup in the dressing room I got to talking with one of the band members, an older gentleman dressed very smartly in a black tuxedo. I asked him about the finale. He said the band wouldn't be staying for it. They planned to leave just before it began—and if I was smart, so would I! "Get out before it's too late," were his exact words. What could he possibly mean? He would say no more.

I went up to the star to tell her my name, so she wouldn't mispronounce it when it came time to introduce me. She smiled and said, "I'm the star, and when the men see me, they'll forget all about you." Then she paired me up with a six-foot-three-inch dancer. This girl was beautiful and she had a lovely body, only it was a big body. Her can was at least forty-six inches wide, but she was not fat. With my tiny, five-foot-four-inch frame, we were a pair that could beat a full house. She was wearing a glittering gown. I thought it quite odd that she had western boots underneath it. She said she'd forgotten her high heels. I later found out she was a transsexual. She'd had a painful and costly operation to become a woman, but her feet remained big and masculine—that's why the boots.

It was not our time to go on yet, so I had to wait in the large dressing room with the other dancers. I sat in a large, pretentious chair with lions' heads for armrests. I took in everything from the pink, crystal chandeliers to the fact that men were now shifting into the dressing room. David had been told to wait out in the lobby. There was one man who seemed to be in charge. He was about forty-eight, potbellied (what else?), sweaty in the face and had greasy black and gray hair. He was hyper. I noticed him huddling with each dancer, the girls nodding dumbly. Eventually he strode up to me. I didn't move from my seat. My hands stayed stretched out on the lion heads. I looked him in the eyes. I did not like, or trust, this man.

He said to me, "Step over here, babes. I gotta talk to ya." I hate men who call me "babes." It's too close to Babs, a nickname people used to call me, which I always loathed.

When I stood up to talk to "Slick," he grabbed me by my arm and squeezed it hard, then said to me, "I expect a rough show out there, got it? You treat these men good, and don't miss the grand finale. You're gonna be very popular." Then he pinched my rear end. A light finally went on in my head. Now I knew what all this finale stuff was about. I was scared and mad. I wanted answers, but everyone was tight-lipped. I went into the ladies' room feeling nauseated. There I saw a stripper performing a sexual favor on one of the conventioneers. I went back to my lions'-head chair. The man came out of the ladies' room, tucking in his shirt and looking guilty. I was livid. I stormed into the ladies' room, grabbed the stripper by the arm, and slammed her into the stalls. I shook the hell out of her and demanded to know what was going on. She was scared. She'd never seen this side of me. I was always the sweet, quiet girl who never made waves. Now I was crazed.

In a shaky voice, she told me that the ten of us were to perform our acts as planned. Then we were supposed to walk out on stage in the nude—and sexually service all four hundred men! Ten of us for four hundred men!

I ran out to the lobby to find David, but he'd been shuffled into the party room. He was one of the sea of faces. And now it was time for me and the giant to go on. I was cooling off and gave in. I decided to split right after the show, skipping the finale.

Our music started. It was live, but we could hardly hear it. I recognized the song, "The Blues in the Night." It could have been a great time if the herd of idiots hadn't been so loud and rowdy. I walked out onto stage all glitter and feathers. I walked all the way down to the end of the makeshift stage while my partner danced up the other end. Then we were supposed to turn around, passing each other going the other way on this narrow stage. I saw my partner barreling down the runway like a train, those wide hips swinging, and I knew she would knock me off the stage into the crowd.

The hard, white lights were blinding me. The men were grabbing my ankles, tearing at my feathers, and confusing me with flashbulbs. As my partner came near, I froze and closed my eyes. I thought I was a goner, but I wasn't. Miraculously, she slipped right by me in cloud of perfume. Soon the act was done. I got off the stage and ran through the lobby of the hotel, naked, with my costume in my hands. I'd forgotten this was a hotel, not a burlesque theater. You should have seen the faces of the people getting off the elevators. I didn't mean to force my nudity on these poor unsuspecting people, but I was preoccupied with getting out before party time.

I found David and explained what was going on. He helped me pack my bags, and the two of us slipped out the back door, running two steps at a time before the thugs the organizers had hired could catch up with us. We ran all the way to the car and tore out of there. We were safe.

David is a pretty rough character, but we were outnumbered. Plus, those thugs carried blackjacks and maybe worse. I left without pay, but that didn't matter. What mattered was that I was safe.

The next day at the burlesque theater, my boss came up to me and apologized for what had happened the night before. Then he paid me my one hundred dollars. He said he thought I'd earned it—I was told I only had to dance.

One day David bought me a book on Marilyn Monroe. I was particularly taken by the famous calendar shot of Marilyn stretched out nude on mounds of red velvet. It was the most tasteful, perfect, artistic photo I had ever seen. From that moment on I was determined to duplicate that shot with me as the model. Now I knew what else I had to do to improve my looks. I had to become a blonde.

I did it—and as a blonde I found doors flying open that had previously been closed to me. Modeling jobs started to come more frequently. I couldn't understand it. I was the same person, with merely a different color hair. I found out the old cliché is true. Gentlemen do prefer blondes. Maybe they think blondes are naturally dumb, and therefore easy. The only thing dumb about becoming blonde is putting all that bleach on your head. That's dumb!

The Marilyn Monroe book left me hungry for more, so I read everything I could about her. I became an expert on Marilyn Monroe, and I came upon some eerie parallels between her and me. Her real name was Norma Jean Baker. My real name is Barbara Ann Baker. Marilyn's height was five feet, four inches. That's exactly how tall I am. Her measurements were 38-25-38. My measurements are 38-25-38. Marilyn's first husband's name was Jim. My first husband's name is Jim. She had an Aunt Grace. I have an Aunt Grace. Marilyn's father's name was Jack Baker. My father and brother's names are Jack Baker. The strangest parallel of all is that an agent by the name of David March introduced Marilyn to Joe DiMaggio. My husband and manager is named David March. These similarities left me a little dazed.

In addition to coloring my hair, I started sporting Marilyn's famous beauty mark. I had my hair cut like hers and did my makeup like hers. As a result, I started getting recognition as Marilyn. I was never told I looked exactly like her. I was always compared to Marilyn Monroe and someone else, usually Mae West or Barbara Eden. One person summed it up by saying that I looked Monroe-ish.

"Keep your butt off the canvas!" These were the words of Manny Rosen. I first met Manny at the Harmony. I had just finished a show, pinned up my hair, and gone out to the lobby for a soda. Sitting across from me was an older gentleman autographing pictures of himself from when he was a professional fighter. He was completely surrounded by girls. They loved him. He was making them all laugh. I observed his magnetic power. When the crowd cleared, it was just me and this character, eyeball to eyeball. He looked at me and said in a deep, rough voice, like Marlon Brando when he played the Godfather, "You want a neck rub?" My first impression was, if he puts one hand on me, I'll kill him. Then he continued, "I know how to give neck and body rubs. Come and sit next to me. I won't bite—this time." I don't know why, but I got up and sat down next to him. He'd put a spell on me, and it was love at first sight. Manny Rosen and I became fast friends, and we still are.

Manny is a writer and has written poetry, songs, and stories. His most famous work is a rap song he wrote for a singer James Brown called "King Heroin." The song was very popular, and as a result Manny was invited on to talk shows by Joe Franklin, Mike Douglas, and Johnny Carson. One day Manny escorted a fellow out of the Harmony Burlesque, and that's putting it mildly. He was seventy-eight at the time. He still works out every day. His arms are well developed, and his chest is very hard. I once remarked, "Hey, Manny, your chest is so hard. Is that from lifting weights, or is rigor mortis setting in?" To which he said, "I'll give you something hard." Manny is still pretty rough.

Anyway, one day I noticed three young men in the theater heckling a dancer on stage, totally ruining her performance. I walked up to these guys and told them to sit down and be quiet, or I would have them thrown out. One of them, a tall, very handsome guy who looked astonishingly like Robert Chambers, looked down at me and said, "We're slumming." He obviously didn't take me seriously and kept on calling the dancers names. I went out to the lobby to get a bouncer, but they were nowhere to be found. Only Manny was watching the door. Manny asked me what was wrong. I told him about these wiseguys heckling the dancer. Manny got up and went inside to see for himself. He then walked up to the big guy, grabbed him by the elbow, and applied just the right kind of pressure. Manny then lead him out the door and told the bunch of them to get out.

I shared a dressing room with a transsexual for a while and never even suspected. A transsexual is a man who undergoes a sex-change operation to become a woman. This operation is both painful and costly. It takes time to complete, and it doesn't always turn out well. Transsexuals are very misunderstood. Many people call them freaks, or homosexuals, or, the favorite description, "mutilated men." In fact they are none of these. Transsexuals are very common in the burlesque circuit. It is often impossible to tell who they are.

My transsexual roommate was beautiful and had a body I'd kill for. She told me she had six children, which astounded me— her body was flawless. Well, it turned out she did have six children, only she was the father.

I'm always surprised to find out how willing transsexuals are to talk about their lifestyles. Before they begin the sex-change process, they have to undergo a battery of tests to determine if they truly have more female characteristics than male psychologically. If they do, they can start taking female hormones to develop breasts and lose facial hair. Their skin starts to get softer, and their bodies become more rounded than squared off. This is called the pre-op stage. While in this stage many transsexuals dress like women, wear make-up and wigs, and look sensational. There's only one difficulty—they still have a penis. Some of these pre-ops become strippers, and they can go over very big. The money goes to their final operation. When the operation is complete, it can be next to impossible to tell them from biological females. Working with transsexuals so much, I've learned to recognize things that give them away. Sometimes they have deep or husky voices, sometimes a big Adam's apple. But the biggest giveaway is that transsexuals are never bitchy or catty and never suffer from monthly depressions so common to women.

Transsexuals are very nice people. I'm happy there is an operation to help them feel better about themselves. They say it is very frustrating to be a woman trapped in a man's body. I guess so! If it were me, I wouldn't like the feeling. We must put ourselves in their place. The world is too quick to condemn. If my son felt trapped in the wrong body and wanted to change his sex more than anything, he would have not only my support, but I would help finance the operation for him. My love for my children is unconditional.

It is true that many exotic women are lesbians. A few strippers in the burlesque theaters I worked in were lesbians. Why are so many exotic women lesbians? It's simple. Many exotic women, be they prostitutes, strippers, go-go girls, porno actresses, belly dancers, or private dancers, have a dislike and mistrust of men. Many of these girls have been married to men and suffered terribly at their hands. Many of these women were battered housewives at one time, or sexually abused. You don't have to be born a lesbian—you can become one. After years of hearing lies and being run into the ground by the wrong type of man, many women find peace in a relationship with another woman. A lesbian lover is often more understanding than a male lover, and more considerate. This, however, is not always true. There are, of course, violent lesbians, too. Remember, no matter how masculine they are or how tough they act, lesbians are still women, and it's human nature for women to have a jealous streak in them. "Hell hath no fury like a woman scorned."

Lesbians are condemned by society and often lose their children to their ex-husbands. They are considered unfit mothers and bad influences on their children. This is totally false and very sad. Lesbians can be wonderful mothers. Their children love them. Lesbianism is a sexual preference—it has nothing to do with children or the raising of them. What goes on behind bedroom doors, be it heterosexual or lesbian, has nothing to do with motherhood. I won't say lesbian lifestyles are right or wrong. I'm not on this earth to judge. But I do say that a woman's sexual preference is her own business, as long as no one is getting hurt or being forced into something she doesn't want to do.

I'm friends with many lesbians. Contrary to popular belief, they do not try to rape you. They are very low-key people who, believe it or not, have other things on their minds besides sex. Without being a lesbian myself, I've been welcomed into the lesbian world. I've danced for lesbian groups on several occasions and found them to be very responsive and wonderful audiences. I wish all my audiences were as enthusiastic.

I once knew a lesbian who for years wanted to have a penis. After tests by various doctors, she was finally able to arrange to have a penis sewed on. She looked like hell, but she was functional. She got the penis erect by squeezing a little ball hidden behind the testicles that inflated a rubber tube in the penis. This woman even got to keep her vagina, and she was very proud of the fact that she had both. She/he worked in Times Square as a hooker, and made more money from straight men than the female hookers did. In time, though, she became disillusioned with being part male and went back to have an operation to be a woman again. This time she was butchered. The operation left her a freak. She had to be sewn up completely, and her vaginal area was cauterized. Her career was over. Later, she was found in her bathtub with her wrists slit.

Times Square has many homosexuals. Homosexuality is oftentimes confused with pedophilia—sex with children. Homosexuals will tell you they have sex with other adult men, not children. The thought repulses most of them. Homosexuals fall into two categories for me. One is the prissy little pain in the ass who hates women. He is usually a makeup artist, hair stylist, or art director who makes your life miserable. The other category of homosexuals is the sensitive, artistic man with a beautiful soul, someone you can always find a friend in. The disease AIDS is making it open season on homosexuals. We've had the gay lifestyle for a long time without AIDS. Now suddenly we have AIDS. No, I believe it comes from another source, but it hit the gay population the hardest. We have lost many talented men to this dreaded disease, but I don't think we should lay blame on anyone, especially when we really don't know too much about the disease. Think of this disease as robbing us of beauty. Look at our loss when Liberace died. When Liberace died, instead of hearing what a great artist he was, we zeroed in on the fact that he was gay. His sex life was more exciting than his music. We totally disregarded the fact that he was a very kind and generous man who made many contributions to charities. But let's talk about him being a "fag" instead. I prefer to think of Liberace as a great performer who brought much happiness into this world. When he left he took a piece of it with him.

I'm a bit of an expert on Oscar Wilde. For those of you who don't know him, Oscar Wilde is a very famous Irish poet and playwright of the nineteenth century. He was also gay. He brought beauty and romance to us. He is the author of *The Picture of Dorian Gray, The Canterville Ghost, The Importance of Being Earnest,* and a host of other marvelous writings. Oscar Wilde saw beauty in all people. However, in the nineteenth century it was not in your best interest to be gay, or, as they called it back then, "a dandy." He was sent to prison for it, and his beautiful spirit was broken. One can tell the difference in his poetry. Before he went to prison, his poems were flowery. In and after prison, his poems were bitter and depressing. Once a famous and beloved poet, Oscar Wilde died a broken and lonely man in France at the young age of forty-eight, all because people preferred to talk about his sex life instead of his contribution to the world.

Prostitutes are the biggest victims of Times Square. They get beat up by their pimps. They get beat up by their johns (customers). They get arrested. They catch a lot of flack from society. Then why be a prostitute? Many girls aren't trained to do anything, so they slip into the oldest profession. This is not to say prostitutes are stupid—far from it. You don't just wake up one morning and say, "I think I'll be a prostitute." Your hand is often forced one way or the other due to financial problems. According to my prostitute friends, after the first time you have sex for money—like it or not, you just crossed the Rubicon—there's no turning back. You think, "Gee, that was easy money." Then things snowball. Before you know it, you're in the business. Some girls don't go about it that way. They get turned out by a pimp. Teenage runaways are the usual girls to get involved with pimps. They are scared and turn to the pimp for comfort and protection. The pimp gives you all you want, for a price—your soul. A pimp is a man who lives off young girls. He procures all the men for the prostitute, then she turns her hard-earned money over to him. She is given a quota for the day, say, two hundred dollars a day. If she doesn't meet her quota, she can either work on into the night or get a beating from her pimp. These girls usually work for twenty dollars a john, meaning they must have sex at least ten times a day, sometimes more, to meet their quota. Now, I know, you've heard this before at any party: A couple of women get a little tipsy and start discussing in slurred voices how they should be prostitutes, they'd get one hundred dollars a man. It's not that easy. It's like pulling teeth to get twenty, let alone a hundred dollars. Many women also think all you have to do is have straight missionary sex. That's not always the case. There are some pretty kinky men out there. And a prostitute can get hurt, maimed, or even killed. Prostitution may seem like easy money, but it's not. You soon lose your soul to it, leaving you a bitter, lonely, and very distrustful woman.

Working in Times Square, I got to know prostitutes. This was no easy feat. Like I said, they trust no one. The black prostitutes hated my white, blonde looks, and the white prostitutes hated me on general principles. When they got to know me, however, they liked me. I'd stop to talk to them on my way to work in the burlesque theaters. After a while they looked forward to seeing me. Some even confided in me. When I played at the big burlesque theaters, with my name in lights and a large poster of me in the window, they'd come to watch. After my performance they'd come to my dressing room to visit. I liked their visits. Sometimes they would bring me fresh strawberries. Prostitutes are not bad girls. Under the hard exterior they wear as a protection you'll find very lonely ladies. It took me some time to get past those hard shells, but, when I did, it was worth it. You'll never hear me put down a prostitute. I'm just glad I don't have to work the streets.

"Porno people are scum!" I've heard that statement on more than one occasion. Why are they scum? Well, because they have sex on stage live, or they have sex in magazines, or they have sex on film. It never seems to occur to people that if there was not such a big market for pornography then all these people would be out of business. Who orders the porno movies? Not the porno people, that's for sure. When they watch television, they watch reruns of "Lassie" or "Star Trek." The very people who condemn pornography are often the first in line to buy up the latest X-rated videos.

I know a lot of porno stars and they are very nice people. When you visit them in their homes they are very hospitable. They can't do enough for you. No, they do not walk around naked and try to talk you into an orgy. They are like anyone else, only more straightforward and honest. Pornography is their line of work, that's all. I have been on porno movie sets to watch, and I can tell you these people are very professional. There is no horsing around at all. There are no drugs on the set. The porno people are very considerate about the actors' feelings. The atmosphere is calm and relaxed. It takes a lot of work to make a porno movie. I'm neither for porn or against it. I'm for the right to watch adult films if you so desire. If it's not for you, then I respect your rights as well. I don't believe porno is responsible for crime. We had crime long before we had porn. Jack the Ripper did very well without porno movies. Porno movies are considered to be disgusting and a bad influence on our children. I, for one, think porno movies are boring and sometimes silly with the diddly-ass music they play in the background. The writing is amateurish and the acting weak. The only thing done well is the actual sex. This can be educational to people who are sexually ignorant. You'd be surprised how many men have been sticking their penises into belly buttons or rolls of fat. They wonder why they can't get their wives pregnant—a porno movie can show the way. I've seen so many porno movies I'm afraid I've become blasé about them. Still, I do not find them disgusting or dirty. Porno movies usually show people making each other feel good.

What *is* disgusting is the new wave of horror films out now, the *Nightmare on Elm Street*-type movies. I've seen veins ripped out of teenagers' bodies, children hung up from meat hooks, and every other conceivable bloody act in these movies. The films actually make me feel faint. Still, we allow our children to watch these atrocities. I would think these movies would be more damaging than X-rated movies. I'd rather have my children go out and make love than go and pull someone's veins out of his body.

So far I've had only good things to say about the people of Times Square. You probably expect me to say something good, or at least tolerant, about Time Square's pimps and pushers, too. Well, this is what I have to say about them. Pimps ruin people's lives and drug pushers murder people. Pimps and drug pushers are boils on the ass of society. There is no good in any of them. They are the part of Times Square that has killed it.

While in Times Square I witnessed a gradual decline of interest in watching women. This is due to drug abuse. A person dependent on drugs thinks first and foremost of his next score. Everything else in his life is secondary—food, family, and sex. Women stripping means very little to drug people. Sometimes they came in, but it was usually just to get warm or to meet a pusher. They cared less about what was going on up on stage. I have no use for drugs or people who use them. I will not do business with drug abusers. Because of them burlesque is gone, and many of the great dancers in burlesque are gone with it.

In my opinion, all the pimps, drug pushers, crooked television evangelists, and child molesters aren't worth a damn and can take a slow boat to China.

I have never done drugs. This does not make me better than anyone else, but it does make me smarter. A lot of people have told me I was lucky not to get caught in the drug scene, but luck had nothing to do with it. I was simply never interested in, or even a little bit curious about, drugs. What I did, anyone could do. I simply said no.

Contrary to popular belief, no one pushes drugs on you. When you say no, that's cool. Sometimes you even get a dopehead's respect by saying you don't want to do drugs. You make them feel like idiots for doing drugs. People don't want to share drugs with you because they like you. They want you to do drugs with them to condone their own drug use. Like drinkers, they hate to get high alone.

One pretty dancer I knew suffered a nosebleed out on stage. Right in the middle of her act, blood dribbled out of her nose all over her naked body. She couldn't control it and ran off stage to the dressing room. I watched her as she trembled all over, wiping the warm red liquid off her face and body. When she calmed down she felt she owed me an explanation, maybe because I saw her snorting cocaine before her show. "This happens sometimes from coke," she told me. As I took one more look in the mirror to check my makeup, my eyes caught hers in the mirror. I said, "If you keep doing that shit, you'll need a plastic surgeon just to blow your nose. Think about it." Somehow what I said made her decide to quit. Later she said that thanks to me she had gotten professional help. She told me she was so much happier clean, not to mention richer. I may not ever do anything great in my life, but I helped her, and that's a lot.

A lot of times these stories didn't have happy endings. One lovely young dancer was the daughter of a very famous person. I'll call her Sue. I met her while I was dancing in Times Square. She was very pretty, well built, and an excellent dancer. She was not so much a stripper as a jazz dancer. Her timing was excellent. She was also hard and bitter. She went out of her way to be tough. No one got near her without getting a barrage of filth. One day I was on stage and noticed her leaning against the wall watching me, her arms folded across her chest. She looked more like a bouncer than a dancer. When my act was over she came up and put a five-dollar bill on the stage as a tip. Then she walked away and yelled, "She's the only damn dancer in this place." Coming from such a good dancer, I was flattered, so I did the unthinkable. I went to Sue's dressing room to thank her. Everyone stayed away from her. She scared them, but I don't scare easy—especially when I could see through that tough façade. In reality, Sue was a frightened young lady. I knocked on her half-opened door. She was sitting huddled in the corner, naked except for athletic socks and sneakers, her head down on her knees.

"What do you want?" she said as I walked in.

I told her I just wanted to thank her for the tip and the compliment.

"Five bucks, big, fucking deal!"

I sat down next to her and told her it wasn't the money that mattered, it was the cry for friendship that brought me backstage.

"Bullshit! I don't need your friendship or anybody! Leave me the fuck alone!"

I wasn't put off by her. We both had about three hours before our next shows, so we talked. At the end of those three hours, I had made a friend who trusted in me.

Sue was a heroin addict. Of course, she told me she could quit anytime she wanted, only she never wanted to. As the months went by, Sue confided in me more and more. She called me "Ma" because she considered my advice sound, although she didn't always take it. She was a runaway. Her father was the celebrity and she hated him. She had never known him, he was now dead, and she didn't care.

One day Sue came racing in, pale and shaken, her hand cupped over her mouth. She pushed past us and tried to make it to the garbage can in the corner of the room, but she didn't make it. She threw up all over us. All the dancers ran out; I went to the ladies' room to get paper towels. When I came back, Sue was kneeling on the floor on her hands and knees, trying to clean up the mess with a Kleenex. She kept saying, "I'm sorry," and "I'll clean it up." I helped her up. I got the janitor to clean the room. I took Sue to the ladies' room and washed her up in the sink. I took her back to my room. She was trembling all over. I got her dressed and I did her show for her. I asked her if she had a stomach virus, or maybe it was something she ate. But, sadly Sue said, "Ma, it was the heroin. Sometimes it makes me sick." She would come to me when she was scared. I'd rub her head in my dressing room. I'd try to talk her into professional help, but she'd say, "Get off my ass, Ma." She borrowed money from me. "Ma, I didn't eat today, can I have ten dollars? I'll pay it back." I gave her the money until I found out she was buying drugs with it. It broke my heart to tell her no the next time she hit me up for money. When she told me it was for something to eat, I offered to take her to dinner. She narrowed her eyes and said, "Fuck you!" and left. Sue started getting pathetically thin and finally got too weak to dance. She started street walking. I lost all contact with her until one day I was headlining at a theater in Times Square, and she saw my picture in the window. I was talking to the ticket taker when I saw a very skinny girl weaving down the hall toward us. When she got up to the ticket booth, I hardly recognized her. Her face was all sunken in. She had huge dark circles under her eyes. Her thin arms were all bruised.

"Hi ya, Ma, how ya doin? Long time, no see. Ya got ten dollars, Ma?"

"No."

"Never mind. I'll see ya, Ma."

She staggered away. I never saw her again. I heard she died of an overdose.

Most addicts will tell you it's next to impossible to get off drugs. But it can be done. Many people have done it, but no one says it's easy. One person who beat her habit was a close friend I'll call Jocelyn. I grew up with Jocelyn on North Fourth Street. We go back more than twenty years. I first met her when she was only five years old, not even in school yet. I was four years older, all of nine.

Jocelyn was a cute little girl who always wore glasses. I was a homely little girl with buckteeth. We were both underdogs, forever being called names by the other kids like "Four Eyes" and "Bucky Beaver." We became very good friends. Sometimes we were the only friends we had. As a result, eventually we became inseparable.

We grew up in the innocent early 1960s. Jocelyn lived upstairs from us, so our families were like one big family. No one stood on ceremony. We were not always buddy-buddy, though. We had our share of squabbles, just like sisters. We went through phases: Barbie dolls, hula hoops, dodge ball, and skateboards. We were partners in double-dutch and we were good! We were partners in hopscotch. We gave little shows in the backyard and sold Kool Aid together.

When she was seven years old and I was eleven, we became official blood sisters. It happened one day while we were eating lunch in the backyard. It was a lovely summer day. Flowers and bees were all over the garden. We really were inseparable, so I decided to make it official. I pulled a long thorn off our rose bush and stabbed my finger harder than I had intended to. Blood gushed all over the place. Jocelyn looked on in wide-eyed innocence. I told her to give me her hand. She pulled her thumb out of her mouth—she was a chronic thumb-sucker—wet and wrinkled from sucking on it all day. I stabbed her finger, too. She didn't cry. She opened her mouth really wide, like a lion, but no sound came out. I told her, "If we mix our blood together, then we will be blood sisters forever." We did.

When our bodies started developing, we compared our breasts and checked to see who was getting more hairs under her arms and elsewhere. Together we started half a riot down at the projects when we were taken by a neighbor for a walk and ended up in a den of hookers. Our moms came down to the project and tore the place up looking for us.

In the late 1960s we drifted apart. Jocelyn went the way of the hippie movement, and I opted for the glamorous life of salesgirl and part-time topless dancer. We had nothing in common anymore. Jocelyn had a whole new set of friends and eventually got involved in drugs. I had my own friends and couldn't understand why Josh would do drugs. I tried to talk to her and tell her she shouldn't fool around with drugs, but she would just look at me and say, "Who's foolin?" Jocelyn was totally rebellious and told me to get off her case, she knew just what she was doing. She was the only kid on the block to attend Woodstock—and she was only thirteen years old! I gave up. Jocelyn's mother couldn't talk to her either. This was a journey she would have to take on her own, and she did.

Jocelyn started out sniffing model glue. This was done by putting the glue in a "Number 2" paper bag, covering her nose and mouth with it, and getting high. She once hallucinated that she saw a lawn jockey in the paper bag taping up the inside. Next she started smoking pot. Jocelyn prided herself on never smoking cigarettes, but she smoked pot. She also tried LSD at a young age. Once she had a bad trip in a park. She took a tab of LSD and then started crawling back and forth in one of those big playground cement pipes. She was panicked because she imagined she was trapped. She did this for twelve hours, until the LSD wore off. She found herself scared and alone sitting on the floor of the big cement pipe. Another time she had a bad trip and imagined spiders crawling out of the air conditioner and coming at her.

Jocelyn started taking heroin for fun, but eventually she found herself a slave to it. It became a necessity for her to live. She started a life of crime to support her habit—writing bad checks, stealing, even holding people up at gunpoint. She was finally put in jail, where she had to fight to keep from being abused.

Finally, Jocelyn got help. She went cold turkey and got herself straight. She was straight for fourteen years. She built her life up. She became a licensed drug and alcohol counselor, working for the court system and a maximum security prison. She was also an investigator for lawyers. Then Jocelyn worked locating runaways. Recently she became a private counselor and a staff member in a large hospital.

Jocelyn lived in the far reaches of the country for years—then, one day, she came back to New York City. Josh and I were reunited and I met her son.

The girl I shared my dressing room with was always depressed. She had plenty reason to be. She was married, had six kids and her husband was unemployed. To make matters worse, he stayed home all day and drank, then went out all night—picking up men to bring home for her to service for a price! All this plus the housework and correcting the kids' homework.

The Angel was another sad case. She acted tough on the outside, but she was a scared little girl on the inside. One day she had to get an abortion. She was all alone, plus she had a drug habit. There was no way she could keep the baby. She did what she thought was best.

I was surprised to see her show up for work later that day, and she was very sick and weak. After a pathetic performance, she went straight to her dressing room and refused to come out. I was concerned for her. Whimpering was coming from behind her door. I knocked but got no answer. I walked in. The room was dark except for the light that shone in from the hallway. The Angel was doubled over, lying naked on a pile of crinkled costumes and holding her stomach. She was sobbing uncontrollably. I bent down and put her head on my lap and started rubbing it. "The baby was the only friend I ever had," she said. "I wanted to keep it, only I could never take care of it properly. When I was lonely, I'd talk to the baby. I knew it heard me. Now I've lost my best friend. I want to die, too." Then she clenched her stomach harder and started crying hysterically, rocking back and forth in my arms. I held her tightly until she fell asleep. She was like a child.

Several months later the Angel killed herself. They found her in her dim, little apartment, dead from an overdose of drugs. She was clutching a teddy bear she'd bought for the baby when she'd been entertaining thoughts of keeping it. On the wall was a poster of the Angel, heavily made up and decked out in a sequined G-string and two huge feather fans. On the couch lay a childlike figure, minus her fans.

Not all the strippers were hard-luck stories. Our Las Vegas show girl went on to marry a millionaire and retire. The oriental dancer got into porno movies. I went into television and magazines.

But most of the stories were sad. We had a lovely belly dancer stripping with us. She had very big breasts. One day she discovered a tumor the size of a golf ball in one of her breasts. She had to have the whole breast removed, but she wouldn't hear of it. She ignored her doctors, and, eventually, she died painfully.

Cancer of the breast was quite common among the dancers. It was not unusual to see a stripper do a performance with a little piece of bandage taped to one breast, covering a small hole where she'd had a piece of tissue removed for testing. Many strippers lost their breasts, while others chose to lose their lives.

I don't know why so many dancers developed breast cancer. I do know many strippers got implants, and the older strippers had the more primitive silicon injections. Beautiful breasts are very important to a stripper, and implants can enhance your breasts. I don't know if there's a connection between implants and cancer, but all the dancers I knew who died of breast cancer had implants in common.

One of the saddest cancer stories involved a dancer I'll call Grace. Grace was not pretty by any means. She was in her late thirties and had four children and a loving husband who couldn't get work because he was uneducated. Still, she was happy working as a fill-in stripper. Her body was that of a woman who'd had four children and let herself go to seed. She was overweight and flabby. Worst of all, her breasts sagged terribly. Grace hated her breasts. From years of breast-feeding, they had just collapsed. She asked around about implants, but she was afraid to get them. She decided to have a breast lift instead. Now, a breast lift is not the same as implants. The doctor surgically removes excess flesh, then lifts the breasts up to make them firmer. The operation leaves pretty big scars that take over five years to fade. We were all happy for Grace. We knew how much she hated her breasts. A few days after the operation, Grace came back to work. The doctor had done a great job. Grace's new breasts were firm and stood right out from her body. The scars weren't too bad at all. I've seen worse. She planned to use body makeup until the scars healed.

A few months later Grace was dead—cervical cancer. The strippers took up a collection for Grace's family. Grace was the bravest stripper I ever encountered. She worked at the theater almost to the end, until she was just too weak.

One day after my show I came out to the lobby for a soda and some rest and called the kids to make sure everything was alright. Nearby Monique was talking to an older woman, about sixty or so. She was very lined in the face and wore thick, orangey, pancake make-up that only emphasized the wrinkles. She crayoned in her lips in a 1940s cupid-bow pout. Her eyes were done in heavy, black mascara that was smudging under her tired-looking, crystal-blue eyes. The woman's hair was flame-red and thinning. She sat very demurely, smoking a cigarette. Her eyes met mine and she gave me the once over.

I heard Monique say, "You can't stay here. There's no work for you." Then the old woman pleaded, "Please, I was a beauty in burlesque, a big name. I was the toast of the town. She stood up and pulled her tight sweater tighter. "I still have my figure."

"Sorry, but we can't use you!" Monique said. "We have enough dancers. Please go home." Monique walked away, leaving the old stripper standing all alone in the lobby, still clutching her sweater. Tears welled up in her eyes and her lined lips started to tremble. She turned slowly to get her bag, then she spotted me still sitting on the lounge chair. Our eyes locked. She smiled at me weakly and looked a bit embarrassed. Then she said to me, "Don't ever let this happen to you. You're the Queen of Burlesque. I was one, too, when burlesque *was* burlesque. This rinky-dink place never could have gotten me back then. I was great. I've got pictures. I was just like you. Quit while you're ahead. Leave them wanting more, or, some day, you'll see me when you look in your mirror." She left, and I never forgot what she said. All through my burlesque days I got to see just what she meant. There were some strippers who were big headliners in the 1950s and 1960s still doing the same routine to a numb audience. These girls were beauties back then, but now they were, well, a bit more mature. When you find yourself needing more body makeup than usual and softer, dimmer lights, then you should know it's time to hang it up.

One of these older strippers came into my dressing room after one of my shows. She said she wanted to see my costumes. Actually, she wanted to see what I looked like without the aid of the soft, red lights. She looked around at my costumes, and we talked. She told me she had toned down her act so she wouldn't steal the show from me. She could have been the star dancer instead of a filler, you see, but she turned it down. It would have taken up too much of her time, so she had let me be the star. Yes, she was being fought over by two millionaires, too. Each wanted to marry her and give her everything, but she didn't want to marry either one. She wanted to be free, blonde, and twenty-one. Well, she was free, she was blonde, but, as for twenty-one, well, maybe on one leg. In reality, she was in her early fifties, heavy in debt, and supporting teenage children all alone. As for men, the tide wouldn't take her out.

While starring in the large sex emporiums of Times Square, I had the opportunity to observe the "stage mother." One day I got a call in the middle of the week to come in and finish the week out for the "star" stripper. She had had to leave abruptly. I thought the dancer was sick. When I got to the emporium, I noticed an older woman with thick eyeglasses floating all over the place, sticking her nose into everything. She was making everybody nuts. She called the live-sex team "scum," and she called the whole place a "whore house." She was in the process of packing the clothes of the "star" stripper who was leaving on such short notice. It was her daughter. The girl was very pretty—and very young. She stood around nervously while her mother raved. An old man came in and took the bags, and the three of them left faster than a bullet passing through Central Park.

I later found out that the old man was her father and chauffeur. The parents had booked their daughter into the theater, let her work there two and a half days, then acted like they had no idea what kind of place it was, insulted the hell out of all the employees (including me), and left in a huff. Actually, we found it all very funny. We were also all glad they had left. How could they not have known it was a sex emporium? And why did they call it a whore house? There is positively no touching in these places. Everything is visual only, nothing more. I made out very well financially that week and had fun with the "scum" and "whores," myself being one.

One girl was married and had three children. She had a very hot temper. On the side she ran around with an older, married man, and one day she found herself pregnant by him. She decided to keep the baby and tell her husband it was his. She had been doing this all along—none of her children were his. One hot day in the theater, she found out her married lover was cheating on her, with his wife, no less. He came in that day to see her show and took his usual front seat, all smiles and very proud of his stripper girlfriend. She, on the other hand, had tanked up on tequila and was getting hotter by the minute. Her intro came, her music played, and the curtains opened. Out she came, twirling down the long runway. When she got up to the front row, where her lover sat smiling, she pulled out a gun from under her long, silver gown and pointed it right at him. Needless to say, he stopped smiling. Fortunately the girl was stopped by the bouncers and taken away. We never saw her lover again.

One stripper was a little overweight and not very pretty. She didn't strip, she just walked out on stage, naked as a jaybird, carrying a violin. Then she would stand on her head and play "Hold that Tiger." Her breasts were so big they covered her face. This was always good for a laugh, but it was not burlesque.

One girl danced with a wooden leg. She would take it off and wave her stump at the audience. I didn't know whether to laugh or cry when I watched her. Some men walked out. I don't know what motivated these girls. They weren't even trying to be sexy.

All strippers are self-conscious. You have to be, totally naked in front of a bunch of strange men. All you can think of is how you look to them. The strangest things pass through your mind, like, "I never should have eaten that doughnut for lunch." You become convinced it landed on your hips. You worry about the monthly water-weight crisis. Water weight feels worse than it looks. You feel spongy and fat, but your breasts look great.

What do dancers do when they get their period? This is one of the most common questions asked about strippers. Some girls book off, but most continue to dance. Often they use a diaphragm and a tampax and either hide the string or cut it off. They change frequently. I must admit, though, I've seen more than one string fall down into sight.

Some people thrive on dancers' self-consciousness. A plastic surgeon used to come around to watch the shows. When the show was over, he'd say to the dancers, "You would look so much prettier with a nose job," or, "Your breasts are so flabby," or, "You need a little nip and tuck in the tummy," or "A face-lift would take years off you." After he'd totally reduce you to a mass of jelly, he'd hand you his card and be gone. He got a lot of business that way. I always thought he was insensitive and totally unprofessional. Some girls found it impossible to perform after talking to him.

In between my dancing, I was doing modeling jobs, mainly for men's magazines, posters, and record jackets. My nose job and my blonde hair were paying off. I had leverage now and refused to take any bullshit from photographers. If I didn't like the photographer, I left. My photos always sold and the photographers knew that working with me meant money. Most of the magazines gave me good photo spreads, but some were awful. One took a set of lovely photos of me in a barn atmosphere and superimposed 86-inch breasts on my 38-inch chest. It was a freak show. When I first saw the intended spread I cried. I told them to cut my head out of the photos. I didn't want to be associated with such a rotten spread. At first the head honchos didn't want to do it, but I reminded them that I was a stripper and everyone would know the spread was a fake. They offered me more money, but I refused it. Reluctantly they gave in. My head was cut off, and I was just mysterious "Wanda" with mammoth breasts.

One photographer I worked with, a woman, was a real "wheel" in the business. She lived in a loft in the City. We were going to shoot some advertisements for a men's magazine, but she decided that I photographed so well, and we worked so well together, that we should do a complete nude layout for the magazine instead.

I liked her, she was very professional, and I was impressed with her studio, which was a mass of complicated cameras and lights.

She told me what kind of costume to get for the shoot—a burgundy satin nighty and several yards of pale-pink, satin material. I would, of course, be reimbursed for what I spent when we got paid for the shoot. I went from dress shop to dress shop, from boutique to boutique, and from one sleazy Times Square lingerie shop to another before I finally found a burgundy satin nighty. It cost me plenty.

I was excited about the shoot. We scheduled it for the weekend. On Friday night I called to confirm the shoot and see if she needed anything else. She answered in a thin, almost inaudible voice, "Yvette, is that you? I'm sorry but I'll have to postpone our shoot tomorrow. I got pinkeye and I can hardly see. Call me in a week and we'll reschedule it, O.K.?" I was very disappointed, but I did know these things happen. I waited a full week, dancing every day and practicing different poses every night in front of my full-length mirror. I called my photographer and inquired about her health. She said, "Yvette, now I have pinkeye in both eyes and I'm almost blind. Call me in another week, O.K.?" One more week went by. I called "Pinky" up to discuss our shoot, and this is what I got: "Oh, hi, Yvette. My eyes are better now, but I'm afraid we can't shoot until I get back from Maine. My father is ill, and I'm going to take care of him. Let's shoot in two weeks, on the fifth at 10:00 A.M., O.K.?" Two more weeks passed by. I canceled my dancing engagements for two days—the day before the shoot, so I would look well rested in front of the cameras, and, of course, the day of the shoot. I called the photographer at 9:00 A.M. the day of the shoot to tell her I was on my way. This is what I got: "Yvette, listen, I'm sorry, but we can't shoot today. I had a dream last night that my cats got feline leukemia from your cats. It was on your shoes when you walked in my studio. I believe this was God's way of telling me not to do a nude spread. Plus my boyfriend says I'm exploiting you by photographing you in the nude, and I wouldn't want to do that. Sorry."

I was livid to say the least. Just when I thought that I had heard it all, this nut comes along. I didn't want to see her ever again, but I had to go back for some costumes I left on my last shoot. I popped over to retrieve my belongings on a Saturday night. Her building had no doorman or security guards. It was a very old, warehouse-type building. People worked on the other floors during the week. My photographer was the only one there on the weekends. A rickety old elevator took me to her fifth-floor studio. The halls were dark and scary. I gathered my few things. There was very little conversation between us. She knew I was pissed, but I remained civil.

Just as I got to the elevator, the door slowly and silently opened. I never did like elevators. If possible I take the stairs. I have an unnatural fear of elevators and getting stuck in one, or having the cable snap and send me crashing to my death. I walked in with mistrust. The door slowly closed. It was a cramped elevator, with one tiny, dim light on the ceiling. I pushed the button for the lobby. The elevator did not move. I pressed again. It stood still. I pressed the button for the door to open. Like before, nothing happened. Suddenly, all my fears came to the surface. Feeling closed in, I started to panic! I hit all the buttons, I pushed at the thick, steel door, then I punched it and kicked it. I started to break out in a sweat. I screamed for help, but no one came. It was the weekend. I was alone. I envisioned myself found dead Monday morning from suffocation. Then a dumb thought came to me—at least I would be found in full makeup. I pounded on the door and screamed until my throat was hoarse. Then I shoved my long, red fingernails into the slight crack in the door. Using my feet for leverage, I pulled at the crack and pushed off with my feet. Suddenly the door flew open, throwing me on my ass. I scrambled up and ran out. I flew down the five flights of dark stairs. I ran out into the cold night air.

As I slowed down to catch my breath and gather my thoughts, I did have one consoling thought. Maybe that bitch would get stuck in the elevator, too.

One day I managed to get a job posing for a biker magazine. Unfortunately, the editor prided himself on being a sleazeball. He was short, fat, and arrogant. I really wanted to be on the cover of the magazine, and I told him so. He told me that I could be on the cover. They'd take the pictures at a car show in New York City.

I was beside myself with joy.

The day of the shoot came. There was a makeup girl to do my face. I don't like to be made up by anyone, especially makeup artists (I use the term loosely). I didn't want to spoil my chances of getting on a cover, though, so I went along. As expected, the makeup girl was a pain in the ass. First, she remarked that my skin was dry. Then she studied my face for an eternity, grimacing all the while. If I had any confidence, she was going to make sure it was gone before the shoot. As she was making me up, she stopped periodically to take a swig of orange juice loaded with vodka from a large orange juice bottle. By the time she was through, I was feeling loaded from her breath blowing in my face.

Needless to say, she made me look terrible. I should have washed my whole face clean and started over, but I had no time. The photographer was supposed to meet me in ten minutes, and it would have taken at least twenty minutes to scrape off the graffiti that had been painted on my face.

I shouldn't have worried about it. Three hours went by and no photographer. My makeup was wilting. Nowadays, I wouldn't wait five minutes, but I was new and didn't want to rock the boat. Finally the photographer showed up. He was stoned out of his wits, but the magazine editor was sweet as he could be to him, bordering on kissing his ass. I would have fired the bastard on the spot.

The photographer took a series of shots on two different Harleys. I had a hard time posing because my face did not match my smile. The way the makeup artist put my lips on made my smile look like a sneer. Crowds were watching the shoot too, since it was in the middle of the bike and car show. I wore two costumes. One was a gold lamé bikini, and the other a pair of ripped shorts and a torn t-shirt with Harley wings sewn on the front. The lights were hot; I felt dizzy and hungry. I never eat the day of a shoot, because it makes a little bump in your belly that is perceptible in photographs. In fact, I starve myself all week. After the big shoot I pig out. I was feeling self-conscious from all the people staring at me. I knew I didn't look my best. My lips were the color of dried blood.

When the shoot was over, the editor told me the photos would be done in a couple of days and that when he selected the cover shot he would call me.

The day finally came. The editor called and said the photos were great. If I wanted to see a preview of the cover, I was to meet him for dinner in New York and he would bring it along. I was so excited I almost exploded! I told everyone who could understand English that I was going to be on the cover of a magazine.

That night I met the editor at the appointed restaurant. We had dinner and dessert, then he said to me, "Would you like to see your cover now?" I responded like a schoolgirl with a giddy "Yes!" He produced a black-and-white xerox copy of my cover. It looked great! I was so happy I almost cried. Then he took my hand and said, "If you really want this cover, what are you prepared to do for it?" My heart sank. I couldn't believe my ears. The old casting couch was rearing its ugly head even in the magazine business. He told me if I wanted this cover badly enough, I'd sleep with him that night. If not, he was going to scrap it. He told me that all the cover girls had to sleep with him, or they didn't get on the cover of his magazine.

The situation required some fast thinking on my part, but I pulled it off. I told the sleaze that I would go out and celebrate with him the day the magazine hit the stands. We'd have a real party, just the two of us, and this way he would know that I was with him because I wanted to be, not just because I was using him to get on a cover. The dumb shit bought it. The magazine came out, I had my cover, and I never saw the son of a bitch again.

Another one of my first cover shots went just about the same way. I wanted to get on covers more than anything, and the editor of this particular magazine knew it. The shoot was scheduled for 2:00 P.M. at the New York Coliseum. The editor told me, "Be on time!" or no cover. I was going to be photographed by a very famous photographer. I was excited. As I understood it, this photographer was much sought after and picky about whom he shot. He didn't "mind" shooting me. I found that very big of him.

The editor got the world's worst makeup artist to make me up. I had no say in the way she painted me—and when I say painted, I mean just that! She looked like she applied her own makeup with a roller, and she made me look like her twin. I felt sick. Two o'clock arrived. I was there. The editor was there. A crowd of oglers was there. But where was the very important photographer? We all hung around. Time passed. Three o'clock came and went, then four o'clock, then five o'clock. My "expert" makeup job was wilting, although this seemed only to improve it.

Around 5:30 King Shit waltzed in and started checking the lighting. He strolled up to me and shoved a light meter in my face. He had the gall to tell me my makeup wasn't fresh enough. Maybe not, but my mouth was fresh enough. I told him my makeup was fresh three hours ago when we were supposed to shoot! He ignored my snide remark, but the editor called me over and told me I was talking to a super-famous photographer and to stop smarting off to him! I told him, "I don't care how famous he is. As far as I'm concerned, he's the most unprofessional photographer I've ever had the misfortune to know—and I've known some winners!" I was told to hold my tongue or no cover shot. I really wanted the cover, so I clammed up. I let the makeup artist crayon my face some more and allowed myself to be pushed, pulled, and pinned. At last the shoot came to an end.

Four days later I got a phone call from the editor. He told me the photos had turned out great and would I like to meet him for dinner in the city and see a rough print of what my cover would look like. It was the same old routine. We were going to a fashionable restaurant, so I opted for a basic black dress and pearls. (With this combination you can never go wrong.) I arrived on time, but the editor was not there yet. I was escorted to my seat to wait for my dinner date. The door opened and in walked what looked like a panhandler. The editor had never been a clothes horse, but I assumed he'd dress for dinner. Faded jeans and a sloppy t-shirt with a peace sign was not my idea of fashionable. The only reason he'd been let in the restaurant was because he had some kind of pull in the upper echelons. We ordered a very delicious seafood dinner, and the editor was charming, despite his appearance. We were quite the pair—he looked like a sleazy john, and I looked like a hundred-dollar hooker. The editor told me he would show me my cover over drinks at a little place he knew of. When we left the restaurant all eyes were upon us. I was dying from suspense. We had our drinks in a seedy little bar with drug transactions taking place right before my eyes, but finally I saw my cover shot. It did look great. It was only in rough black and white, but I was so happy I was near tears.

Then drops the bomb. "Now that I gave you a cover, what are you going to give me?" I couldn't believe my ears. The almighty "casting couch" had come crashing into my living room for the second time. The editor told me he slept with all the girls he put on the covers—"No sex, no cover." I felt my eyes well up, but I was smart enough to know that if the magazine had gone as far as black-and-white prints of the cover, it was probably too late to stop the presses. I told him he was a sleazeball. He said he knew it and was proud of it. Then I told him to keep his cover, I didn't fool around on my husband, not even for a cover. I was right. My cover came out regardless. "Nice try, ace," or, should I say, "ass."

In the not-so-distant past, nudie magazines depicted only semi-nude women in black and white. These were usually sold only from under the counter or through mail order, and they were always in a brown-paper wrapper. Today men's magazines are sold right out in public in slick color and with total nudity, including the ever-popular "split shots," spread-open vaginas.

Not only can you get total nudity, but there are now magazines for every fetish—only asses, just big tits, mostly feet, some with older women, some with only fat women, only blondes, only oriental women, some with lesbians, threesomes, sadomasochism, some showing gay love, young men only, and whips and leather. If you look in the right places, kiddie porn is still available. It's just gone underground. In my opinion that's where it belongs! With the exception of kiddie porn and beastiality, I don't see any harm in these magazines.

I don't believe that they cause people to commit crimes. I think they merely entertain and incite masturbation. If everyone was at home quietly masturbating, then there would be a lot less crime, rape, and disease.

If this kind of stuff is not for you, then stay clear of it. This is strictly adult entertainment. If you are not adult enough to handle it, then come back when you grow up.

Most modeling shoots are pleasant experiences, that is, if you are a model who has some credibility. If you are new, you are treated like a piece of meat. That's how it was at first when I started modeling, but now I am my own boss. I do my own makeup and hair, and I am in total control of my poses.

The entire week before a shoot I eat mostly salads, Slim Fast, and granola bars with diet soda. I weigh myself every day to make sure my weight is proper. A fashion model has to be very thin, but a nude model needs to be voluptuous and well proportioned. Thin is not in with men's magazines. I exercise more that week than usual, and I go to bed around nine P.M. I do no reading the whole week and use eyedrops twice a day to keep my eyes from being bloodshot. I practice poses in front of a full-length mirror. The night before the shoot I eat and drink nothing at all. I have no breakfast the morning of the shoot, not even coffee or juice. Liquids make you pee, of course, and I am completely covered in body makeup before a shoot, even on my nether regions, so going to the bathroom is not very practical.

Modeling may look easy, but it is often very difficult to achieve the looks a photographer may be after. It's even harder when you are totally naked under hot white lights. You mustn't feel self-conscious or worry about other people on the set watching you. You have to concentrate on the look you want to convey to the camera. In men's magazines you must always look hot and sexed up. Of course you aren't, but you have to act the part. You also have to know your own anatomy and how it works best for you. For instance, turning your arm a certain way will make it look slimmer.

Leaning forward makes your breasts look bigger. You can't scrunch up your neck, or you'll make double chins in the photo.

My back and legs always hurt after a shoot, from all the painful positions I have to get into. So I soak in a hot bath and sip cold champagne. David always has a nice dinner planned—he sends out for pizza or chicken in a bucket.

One shutterbug lunatic was a fat, funny-looking guy who fancied himself the fourth stooge in the Three Stooges. He loved them. All during my shoot with him he played "Three Blind Mice," the Three Stooges' theme song. Then he'd get mad as hell because you couldn't look sexy for the camera. Some mood music!

I've had at least six agents during my career, and I eventually fired them all for being jerks. The first agent I had always wore a religious ring and fancied himself the pope or something. All his clients were supposed to kiss his ring whenever they came into his office. I was new so I didn't take this ritual very seriously, until one day all his girls were summoned to the office for an important meeting. There I witnessed a bunch of show biz hopefuls kissing this agent's ring for the sake of getting the "big" break. Not me. When he offered me his hand I laughed and pushed it away. His face turned bright red. After the meeting the asshole told me that I'd better not ever embarrass him again in front of important people! I'd have to kiss his ring like everybody else, or there would never be any work in show business for me. I told him I would be more than glad to kiss his ring in front of everybody if he would kiss my ass in front of everybody. So ended my professional relationship with him.

Another agent said he wanted to get me into the music business. He said I could sing like an angel, but I knew I had a voice like a cow pissing on a flat rock. All I had to do to become a famous singing star was move in with the guy. Live with him like man and wife. Cook and clean for him. And put out to disc jockeys—that's how I would become famous.

Another asswipe of an agent told me he could get me parts in movies. I went to his office, and he did indeed have photos of himself with famous people hanging all over the walls. His favorite was a shot taken with Brooke Shields. He sat down behind a huge desk and told me to have a seat. He had a huge cigar stuck in his face, and I can't stand cigar smoke. After the usual questions, he excused himself for a moment. Soon he came back naked except for athletic socks and a big yellow towel. He sat back down and told me to continue, but soon he asked me if I would mind crossing my legs while he jerked off. I asked him if Brooke Shields had ever been in his office. He said she had. I asked him if he'd asked to jerk off in front of her. "Of course not!" he answered. So I got up and said, "If you don't do this in front of Brooke, then you don't do it in front of Yvette Paris!" I then left him all alone with his yellow towel and his lily in his hand.

Another idiot of an agent dressed like the Disco Duck, gold chains and all. He cleaned his fingernails with a Chinese star. He told me he was a black belt in karate. In karate you have to work out every day. This guy was a graduate of the School of Who Needs Sit Ups. He told me the way to become famous was through videos. Now, for ten thousand dollars he could make up a professional video starring me and get it played on television for five minutes, guaranteed to get my phone ringing. If I didn't have ten thou, well, he could probably do one for five thou.

While I was increasingly popular in Times Square as a stripper, I still had layovers between star engagements. This is to say, I wasn't allowed to dance in any one place for more than a week. I'd get stale. No matter how well I danced, or how much of a star I was, the men would tire of me. So, I only danced at each place once a month for a week, and then I was off until the following month.

In order to supplement my income, I took other stripping-type jobs. One of these was being a "private dancer," just as in Tina Turner's song. In the Times Square shops that say "Live Nude Revue" or "Nude Girls," there is usually a range of sex-related businesses. They have all types of pornographic reading material, marital aids, and peep shows that show glimpses of X-rated movies for a quarter token (the more tokens you drop, the more of the movie you will see). But up a stairway lit up in bright neon, you'll see staring down at you, luring you on, the private dancer. She's scantily clad in something sexy, usually a French corset and fishnet stockings, standing high on stiletto heels. There may be anywhere from eight to ten private dancers, or, as they are often called, "booth babies." These girls work in rows of booths upstairs, about as big as two phone booths—one for the customer, one for the booth baby—with curtains and bullet-proof glass in between.

The customer walks around and checks out each booth baby, finds one he likes, then gives her a nod. She goes into her booth, closes the curtains, locks the door, and waits. The gentleman in question goes in his side of the booth, drops a dollar token in a slot, and the curtain opens for one minute. The booth baby gives him a private striptease, just for him—"private dancer."

Unfortunately, the booth baby gets to see some "shows" herself. I must say, being a booth baby was a real eye-opener. I was the girl in Booth E. For five hours a day I got to do private strip shows for lonely men. Worse, the booths were equipped with phones, so the customer got to tell you his fantasies. By the time I left to catch my bus, I was in a daze. I won't go into the fantasies I heard (they are worthy of their own book), but I will say this much: After hearing their fantasies, I can understand why these were very lonely men.

While doing my stint as a booth baby, I got to meet some very nice girls, although, like in burlesque, they didn't treat me very nicely in the beginning.

First of all, I was about the only white, blonde booth baby. Most were black girls. When I arrived on the job, they treated me as if I wasn't there. They didn't know what to make of me. Some thought I was a narc. They would all be talking and laughing in the dressing room while doing their makeup and getting ready for a day's work, and then I would walk in they would suddenly fall silent. They wouldn't let me use the makeup table and wouldn't give me a locker to keep my things in, so I had to change in my booth and keep my bag there, too. It was very lonely for me working there during that period. There is nothing more humiliating than trying to talk to someone or trying to join in a conversation and being totally ignored. I felt like crying, but I was determined to make them like me.

We were allowed to have a half-hour break, but many girls passed it by to make more money. I never left the floor either. Instead, I'd bring cut-up cheese, Wheat Thins, and a box of juice. I'd eat a little in between shows. The other girls would send someone out for a snack or buy food from Grandma, a little old black lady who traveled to all the sex emporiums and burlesque theaters, carrying a shopping bag filled with fried chicken and tiny, homemade sweet potato pies. She got up at five in the morning to start frying chicken and baking pies. Grandma made out quite well. Even the drug dealers on the streets would buy pies from her. No one bothered her. It was an unwritten rule of the streets to "never hustle a hustler," that is, leave other street people alone. I could walk through Times Square at two o'clock in the morning and cut right through the street people. They wouldn't bother me because they knew I was out hustling the same as they were.

One day I thought up a plan to warm up everybody's cold shoulder. I decided to make extra cheese and crackers. When lunchtime rolled around I unwrapped my cheese pieces, arranged the Wheat Thins, and went from booth to booth offering each girl some refreshments. At first they looked at me as if I was crazy. No one took any, but I told them that if they changed their minds they could just come to Booth E and help themselves. Well, there were no takers, but I persisted. I went through this ritual for a week before I got a response: I went up to one of the toughest black girls, held the cheese platter up to her, and said, "Go ahead, it's good for you. I didn't put any dope on the cheese." That made her laugh. It was the first time anyone had ever seen her laugh. She joked back, "Well, if you didn't put any dope on the cheese, then I don't want it." Now the rest of the girls were laughing, and they finally broke down. They ate the cheese and crackers so fast you'd think they just gotten off a life raft. After that they all came to expect some cheese every day.

They would gather around my booth, and we'd have a little cheese party every afternoon.

We became very close and the girls actually looked up to me for answers to things that bothered them. I got the best locker, and if I walked in and there was no room at the makeup table, the girls made room for me. They even let me bring in my camera and photograph them in their booths. I put all the pictures in a scrap-book and made each girl a copy of her photo. These girls were all sexy, beautiful young things, with extremely hard lives.

The black girl in the booth next to me was especially pretty, with long, lovely legs. She had only one problem—she was six months pregnant. Her stomach wasn't very big, so she continued to work. It was her first baby. I tried to talk to her about prenatal care. Every day she told me about her plans for the baby. Sometimes she'd buy toys for the baby and show them to me.

One day I got to work early. I was the only booth baby on the floor. The disco lights hadn't even been turned on. I was doing my makeup when the pregnant booth baby came limping up the stairs. She was sobbing profusely. She went into her booth and I could hear her crying. I knocked on her door, and, when she didn't answer, I opened it and walked in. She sat doubled over on her stool, her winter hat and coat still on. In between sobs she told me that the baby's father had beaten the hell out of her with a lead pipe that morning. He had been in a bad mood. She took off her hat and took my hand and ran it over a bunch of big lumps on her head. Her face was a mess. Her eyes were swollen and her teeth were loose. She took off her clothes to show me her body. It was all covered in black-and-blue bruises. Her stomach was covered with bruises, too. She cupped her face with her hands and cried her eyes out. I pulled her towards me and hugged her and stroked her lumpy head. She grabbed onto me and buried her face in my breasts and cried until she had no more tears. I got so saturated I had to change my costume. The other girls started coming in. They stood silently outside the booth while I held her. You would think this girl would leave such a cruel man. Well, she didn't. Her baby was born dead. A blessing in disguise? Maybe.

I believe in the right to have an abortion in this sense: A woman should be the one to decide whether she should be pregnant or not. No one else can, or should, make that decision. There are many reasons someone might have an abortion, and thank goodness we have the proper facilities to perform them instead of forcing women to go to back-alley butchers. In the cases of rape, incest, retardation, deformities, AIDS- and drug-ridden babies, teenage mistakes, and financial difficulties, I believe abortion should be an alternative.

But the anti-abortionists have a point, too. I personally know of women who have abortions like they get haircuts at the beauty parlor. They are very cavalier about it. I've heard discussions of upcoming abortions that go something like this:

"Did you have your abortion yet, Wendy?"

"No, but I'm going in on Friday. I'll rest up a day or so, and then I'm off to the mountains with Tom. Isn't it romantic?"

"Well, I had my abortion last week—makes three in all. Oh well, it's for the best. Besides, it's not like it's a living thing, right?"

When I asked them why they don't use birth control, they said, "It's too much trouble. It spoils the spontaneity. Besides, an abortion is no big deal."

Then there's the totally modern couple. They get to choose the sex of their baby. If you find out in advance that the baby you are carrying is not the sex you had your little heart set on, then abort and try again. What could be more simple? Even in cases like these, I do still believe in abortion, for the mere fact that these people would make lousy parents. They are too self-centered to give love to anyone but themselves. But I don't believe they should be granted abortions like haircuts. I think that after two abortions they should be neutered, like you would neuter a bitch in perpetual heat. What about their rights as Americans? In my opinion, they gave up those rights when they decided to make a sport out of a life.

As for me, I could never bring myself to have an abortion. Not for religious reasons, but because I'm a mother of two wonderful children, Jack, fifteen, and Juliet, ten.

Runaways are not as common on the street as popularly believed. There were definitely some, however. One girl in particular shocked even the booth babies. She was young, sixteen at the most, but she had a phony I.D. that said she was twenty-two! These were obtained on the street for a fee. The kid was very pretty, blonde, and had a cute figure—she still had a little baby fat. As hard as she tried to be, she never once fooled the booth babies or me. She wanted to do it all in one day! She knew I was a burlesque star. She wanted to be a burlesque star that very day. Now, she had never even go-go danced in her life, let alone stripped, but she was game. Next she wanted a tattoo. We all warned her against this, but she could not be told. Then she wanted to be a hooker. The pimps would come around looking for her. We told her to stay clear of them, but she thought she knew better.

One day a pimp, all dressed in red leather and a big "sky" hat with feathers, came in to check her out. She was so impressed by his smooth manner and his red leather suit that she left with him despite our warnings. Many months later, I saw her on the street. She had grown up fast. She had gotten into drugs. She had gotten heavy, and her face had tired lines all over it. Incredibly, in the space of just a few months, she had become so spent that the pimps had no more interest in her. She supported herself by turning two-dollar tricks down by the trestle. I once asked her about her mom and dad. She became very hateful and told me that her mom was dead as far as she was concerned and anything in Times Square was better than sleeping with your own father! I couldn't say much to that.

One of the booth babies I became friendly with was a good singer. She looked and sang just like Diana Ross. She, too, was supporting her man by working as a booth baby. She couldn't get night club engagements because he would come along and start trouble in the clubs. This girl was from Haiti, and she was very superstitious. If I hung my coat on a doorknob, she'd cry because it was such bad luck. She told me I should wear a crystal around my neck for good luck. She said she would pick one up for me in her travels.

One day around Christmas she came to my booth with tears in her eyes. She wore a thick woolen hat and scarf and red-and-white-striped mittens. In a shaky voice she told me that her boyfriend had stolen $300 she had been saving for Christmas presents. He took her television and her stereo, too, and he cut up her clothes for good measure. She didn't know where he had gone. Now she would have no Christmas. She turned to go to her booth, but remembered something. She turned back to me and held out a mittened hand. "I almost forgot. Here's the Times Square crystal I promised you. Put it on a chain and wear it in good health." Then she was gone. I never saw her again. I had the crystal put on a chain. When I wear it, it reminds me that I once belonged to Times Square. In spite of all her problems, this girl still remembered me.

The popular feeling seems to be that a street girl is no good. She can never be trusted. She will cheat on you the moment your back is turned. A street girl has no feelings. She is only interested in money and material things. "Watch your wallets"—street girls are sneaky trash.

Well, this is the real street girl: She's as hard as a rock and as jagged as busted glass—on the outside. It is her nature to be mistrustful, particularly of men. She is taught self-preservation at an early age. Will she stab you in the back? Only if she has to. Will she like it? No. She likes flowers. She buys herself a bouquet once a week from the street vendors. She loves animals. She most likely has a cat; an animal is about the only thing she can truly trust. She's mad about stuffed toys and pretty dolls. She likes to read Harlequin love novels with happy endings. She dreams about Prince Charming taking her away from all this. She has a weakness for ice cream, any flavor. She believes strongly in God, but is afraid he is mad at her. Deep inside, street girls are soft and feminine and very childlike, but they'll never let you see that side of them. To show that side of them on the streets could bring them harm.

When street girls finally do fall in love, unfortunately it is with the wrong type of man. A street girl has no self-esteem. She feels the wrong man is the best she can do. Her boyfriend will usually take great advantage of her, perhaps beat her senseless, and eventually move on to greener pastures. Still, she loves him, and she will always take him back. She feels no one else will have her. She thinks she's lucky to have him. Even a bad man is better than no man. Such is the street girl's philosophy. So, the next time someone calls a street girl trash, just remember what I have said: They're angels with soot on their wings.

Being a booth baby was the most demoralizing of all the exotic jobs I had. I had to watch men jerk off and listen to them talk dirty to me for five hours a day, every day. Many of the men who walked into my booth wore expensive, three-piece suits, only for me to discover they wore a bra and garter belt with matching lace panties and stockings underneath them. After a while I started looking at all men and wondering which ones wore lacy undies under their suits. I'm all for fantasies, but some of these guys were sick, homicidal bastards. After seeing men's penises in all shapes, sizes, and colors, after watching various masturbation tricks, after seeing green cum, I was totally fucked up. Before long, when David unzipped his pants to get ready for bed, I started giving him dirty looks. I wanted nothing to do with men or sex.

After listening to dirty talk for so long, I can never tolerate an X-rated phone call at home. I just take a deep breath and totally gross the bastard out. The booths were so bad that I didn't even begin to get my head straight until about three months after I quit working in them.

It has been four years since I left live dancing and the peep booths. My mind is pretty clear now, but it took time. No one leaves the exotic world totally unscathed. People who say they did are lying. When you are exposed to sexual entertainment every day—working the booths, listening to sick fantasies, watching porno movies play continuously, hearing heavy breathing, getting propositioned, being gawked at, being pawed, and seeing men at their worst—you get at least a little bitter, sometimes a lot. I know I did. It did put a damper on my own sex life. I really didn't want to hear anything sexual at home. David suffered for this, but he understood. I was beginning to view him as one of what we girls called the "horn bags." I couldn't distinguish between men. They were all animals.

I got out in time, before I became so bitter or hard that I could not recover. Although I'm out of the exotic world now, the exotic world will never be out of me. I still see things exotically. I can tell how big a man's penis is just by looking at his feet, hands, and nose. I can tell what his kink is by talking to him for an hour. I know who wants to be dominated, who will cheat on his wife, and who likes to drink urine. I wish I was still in the dark about men, but I'm not. I was in the business too long.

Nonetheless, if I had a chance to choose another way of life, I would probably choose the exotic again. I'd rather know what is going on. I would not want to be like so many women who just don't have a clue. The exotic world has affected me in both positive and negative ways.

Because of this innocent/hard personality it has given me, people talk to me as though I were a child, only to stand in shock when I blast them away with a string of obscenities. They can't believe that a nice little girl like me could say such foul things. What they don't know is that men just like them have been my teachers. I'm not a man-hating bitch, but I can see how a girl could become one. As I said, I got out in time.

While I was a booth baby, I also did bachelor parties as a stripper, or sometimes as a belly dancer, depending on what the "bachelors" wanted. What is a bachelor party? It is a party given for a future groom, usually some time in the week before the wedding, by well-meaning friends who get together to give their good buddy one last fling before he walks that last mile. A hall is rented, beer is shipped in by the case, and someone brings X-rated movies, commonly known as "smokers." The friends also pool their money to get a live dancer, usually a stripper.

If the price is high enough, many strippers double as hookers when they do bachelor parties. The groom is put under pressure to have sex with her in front of all his pals. Sometimes the groom will do it, in order to not hurt his buddies' feelings or so he won't be thought of as a fag. He risks all kinds of disease for his friends. Some of these hooker/strippers will also take on any other member of the party who is willing to pay extra. Sometimes the dancers just dance, and hookers are hired for after the show. Not all bachelor parties are like this—but many are.

One time I was hired to dance down by the docks. The party was being held in an abandoned factory. David and I parked on a dead-end street in the shadows of old factories. The street was cobblestone, and at the end of the street was the river. Would you believe it was actually foggy that night? Well, it was. The whole thing was out of a horror movie. I was expecting either Jack the Ripper to come out of an alley or Godzilla to pop out of the water. The factory in question was lit only by dim, naked light bulbs. We went up a staircase, following posters with targets and the word "stag" painted on them. The targets led us to a freight elevator. I went in reluctantly. The elevator slowly ascended the floors. When the elevator door opened, to my surprise, horror, or humor, this is what met my eyes: about fifty grown men standing around wearing Styrofoam pork pie hats with Styrofoam antlers stapled on them. The whole construction was spray-painted black, obviously the same paint used to spray paint the word "stag" on all those posters. I'm not sure just what they were supposed to be—moose, antelope, or reindeer—but I think it had something to do with being virile. To me they looked like Mr. Moose on Captain Kangaroo. As the men stood around watching porno flicks and sucking down beers, pretending this was the time of their lives, I was asked to go to another room.

Inside was the bride along with her mother and father and even the groom's mom and dad! So were all the girlfriends of the antler brigade, working feverishly pasting streamers on a huge, makeshift stripper pop-out cake. I was asked to pop out of this cake. It was made of cardboard covered in white icing from a can (a lot of cans). One girl was cutting pictures of naked ladies out of a girlie magazine and taping them all over the cake.

This was an unusual bachelor party. Never had I seen the bride and her family present. At least I knew it would be safe. All the people turned out to be very nice. The girls took turns trying on my feather boa. I had a hard time getting it back.

Because it was a makeshift cake, there was nothing for me to stand on inside. I stepped into the bottom of the cake, someone put the top on, and then the cake and I were wheeled out into the middle of the party room. When my music started to play I was supposed to pop out of the cake and dance up to the groom. There was just one problem—only my head stuck out of the cake. There was no way I could climb out. So, I popped out my head. I felt foolish listening to my music run, trying to look sexy, and wondering how the hell I would get out. Two alert gentlemen ran to my defense. They pulled me out by my arms and legs. This was not a very pretty sight. I was all covered in white icing. The groom was seated on a chair in the middle of the floor. I danced all around him and sat on his lap. The bride was scrutinizing his face for any signs of emotion, but, I must admit, he was a cool one. He sat perfectly rigid and unaffected the whole time. I could see the sweat all over his face, though. Outside of losing a pair of rhinestone earrings, I did alright that night.

I had been studying at a dance school for a while, and one day I talked the owner into letting me give burlesque dance lessons to the other students. He thought it was a great idea so he gave me a shot at it.

He advertised in a local newspaper. "Ladies, learn how to strip for your husband!" Well, we had takers. I taught them how to have poise, do their makeup, and dress sexy. We didn't strip down to nudity, only to a bathing suit or leotard. You'd be surprised who showed up to learn to strip. I had ladies in their sixties and early seventies. They were really gung ho. Looking at their bodies, I was glad there was no nudity. All in all, it was fun. But I had to give up my teaching because I was too busy dancing. Perhaps someday I'll teach dance again, since it is, and always will be, a big part of my life. There isn't a day that goes by that I don't dance in one form or another for fun and exercise.

One magazine editor thought I could play a part in a porno movie he was shooting. I wanted no part of it, but he told me that I would not have to do anything sexual. All I would have to do was sit at a bar with my movie husband and daughter and be harrassed by bikers, rendered topless, and dragged off the set. Then I could collect $250 and go home. It sounded O.K., so I agreed.

The scene was shot in a bar that was closed for the movie. The main porno stars were Rhonda Jo Petty and Ron Jeremy. The rest were staff of the magazine dressed to the hilt as bikers. It was a fun atmosphere. Everybody had respect for each other. There was no hanky panky going on, and I saw no drugs being used. When an important sex scene was being shot and the man in question had to get an erection on cue, no one laughed or made rude remarks if he didn't rise to the occasion. Everyone kept quiet and gave him privacy. There was no stress on the set. During a break I kidded around with all the make-believe bikers. I took pictures of everybody. I didn't stay long. When I was done, I got my money and left.

Things were deteriorating in burlesque. I noticed subtle changes with every passing day—changes in the management, changes in the dancers, and changes in the patrons. At first I couldn't put my finger on it, but a career I was once very comfortable with began to feel uncomfortable.

Herpes and AIDS were threatening us. Lovely young dancers were feverishly covering up outbreaks of herpes. I saw some girls break down and cry because the herpes was so painful. Sometimes the sores could not be covered with makeup, so the dancer went out on stage with oozing sores. This, understandably, turned off a lot of men in the audience, and soon we were losing our respectful clientele. AIDS was on everyone's mind. Otherwise intelligent men were asking ridiculous questions like, "Could I get AIDS from watching a naked dance?" or, "Could I contract AIDS from watching a porno movie?" Once a guy asked me in all seriousness, "Can I get AIDS if the guy sitting next to me breaks wind and I inhale it?"

The new clientele was not interested in a lovely dancer or glamorous gowns and feather fans. They were more interested in drugs. As for dancing, they only wanted us to do degrading performances on stage. A lot of the girls were getting caught up in cocaine and getting desperate for money, so they did raunchy, degrading acts in order to make tips. I would stand in the darkened wings, watching filthy acts that had nothing whatsoever to do with burlesque. The audience of degenerates showered them with money. The more raunchy you were, the more you made, plain and simple. As I watched otherwise good dancers humiliate themselves on stage, a silent tear ran down my face. I felt the end was near.

Because of all the raunch and drugs that were going down, the police were forever coming in to inspect the theaters. There were a lot of undercover vice detectives. We never knew who was what. In the middle of a show the house lights would go up, and the fire department would burst in looking for a nonexistent fire, completely ruining your performance. I never touched drugs, but I was being watched with everyone else. If there was ever a drug raid, I would be arrested, too. As a result, I was always on edge.

The better dancers were going on the road. The audiences were thinning out. I often found myself dancing for two or three men, with one of them asleep. No one cared about the "Queen of Burlesque" anymore. I was starting to get obscene requests from an audience I no longer recognized. No more did I see Frenchy and his cowboy hat, or the guy with seven hundred dollars in singles and a bag full of sandwiches. There were no more army generals or lawyers, no judges or any other regulars we came to know and have fun with. The girls stopped working on their acts. "What for?" No one cared. One day I said to myself, "What am I doing here? Why am I going on after a raunchy act that left the stage slippery with baby oil?" Burlesque was dead.

I made the decision to quit right there. My last act consisted of my very first strip act. I dressed to the teeth in a black gown and long rhinestone earrings. David and I were the only ones who knew this would be my last performance as a stripper. I stood in the darkened wings waiting for my music. I felt my heart pounding with excitement, as if I was about to start my first performance. I could see the rose-colored lights of the stage. It was a full house that night. I saw my David in the front row. We had come a long way together. How many nights had I seen him sitting in the front row, applauding wildly like all the other patrons? Tonight he looked a little sad. My bags were already packed. Immediately after the show, I would get into my street clothes, walk out of the theater, and never come back.

My music started. The audio man announced me. "Tonight, Yvette Paris. This is the last time she will be seen on stage. Let's hear it for Yvette Paris!" The crowd roared. I was perplexed. How did he know? I made my way to the stage. I felt the warmth of the lights on my face. I felt my music pulsating up my legs and taking over my body. My movements came naturally to me. I looked out at each and every face in the audience and felt their eyes upon me. At the end of my performance, one of my earrings flew off and landed under David's chair. I looked at my David, my eyes were full, and I made a slash across my throat, the sign I gave at the end of a night go-go dancing.

I met a number of famous people while I did burlesque. Among them was the living legend Tiny Tim. Tiny's manager was part owner of the theater I danced at. Tiny loved dancers, and sometimes he would come in to watch a show. He was very generous with tips. The girls loved him.

One day Tiny's manager told me to come to his office and to bring my camera. When I got there, nothing special was going on. So we talked and I sat around listening to a few new tapes. Suddenly the door opened and there was Tiny Tim! He was a giant! I couldn't believe my eyes. I had no idea he was so tall, and because I had never seen him in color (the family couldn't afford color television in the sixties) I thought he had black hair. It was really more of a red. Tiny Tim was very charming. He called me "Miss Yvette." We sat and talked for a few hours. We took a lot of pictures and had a good time all around. Tiny is a gentlemen in every sense of the word. It was my birthday in a week and I invited Tiny to my birthday party. He accepted. When he arrived, he had his electric ukulele with him and insisted on singing all night long. We had a grand time. He sang every song we requested and had an interesting story to go with every one. There isn't a song that Tiny doesn't know. He is an expert on music. But I wasn't going to let him get away without singing you know what—"Tiptoe Through the Tulips." He did, and it was thrilling! Later Tiny read everyone's palm. He used to be a palmist, and he was very accurate. We took pictures and taped the whole party. Then Tiny sang "Happy Birthday" to me.

As the evening was coming to an end, I put my daughter to bed. Tiny went into her bedroom, sat on the end of the bed, and sang her to sleep. Some day she'll realize just how famous that man was who sang her to sleep, but for now he's just the man who sings funny songs.

While getting ready for work one day, David read me an item from the newspaper. Charlton Heston was coming to town to be master of ceremonies at an event called the Scotch Games. I came out of the bedroom and asked David, "Would you like to meet Charlton Heston?" "Sure," he replied. I said I would arrange it. Naturally, David was perplexed.

This is the story. When I was sixteen years old, I worked in a factory outlet that shipped men's shoes, shirts, and pants. I spent long, boring hours in a sweatbox of a room, shipping out shoes and measuring the inner seams of men's pants.

One day I got an order for thirty pairs of shoes in various colors and styles. The customer? Charlton Heston. It was 1968 and *Planet of the Apes* was the big movie of the moment, starring you know who. I had the damnedest time packing the crate full of shoes. When I was done, the manager came to inspect it. In a moment he told me to take the crate apart and pack it again. I was furious, but

I did what I was told. After another battle arranging the shoes, the manager came by again, and he yelled at me to do it over *again!* I was in tears as I redid the job one more time. Finally I got it right.

Later I went to see *Planet of the Apes.* As I sat in the dark theater eating popcorn, I made a vow that one day I would tell Charlton Heston all the trouble he put me through. About two weeks later I was sitting in the factory cafeteria, eating a soggy tuna fish sandwich, when I noticed a black-and-white, glossy photo of Charlton Heston hanging proudly on the wall, autographed to the ladies of the factory. I told my girlfriends that one day I would meet him and tell him the story of the shoe crate. My friends laughed and told me to dream on. When I got home I told my mother the same thing. She laughed and told me that people like Charlton Heston don't talk to people like us, so I should get that notion out of my head.

David and I went to the Scotch Games, which was filled with bagpipes and throngs of people. We had a lot of fun. Then, up on the grandstand, surrounded by hundreds of people, I saw *him.* Charlton Heston was dressed very sharply in a green jacket and kilt. He was addressing the crowds and introducing the next game. I was too short to see through all the people, so David put me on his shoulders. When I had seen enough, David said, "I don't know if you'll be able to get near him." The star was completely surrounded by bodyguards. When he was finished speaking, Mr. Heston was ushered into a trailer for a press conference. Only the press could get in, so I got at the end of the press line and followed all the other reporters in. I was immediately stopped by a tall, ugly man dressed in a high, furry, black hat. "Just where do you think you're going?"

"I'm with the press," I responded.

"Oh really? Where's your press card?"

"I left it in my other bag."

The story was not working. I told the man, "I just have to talk to Charlton Heston," to which he replied, "you and everybody else."

David and I stood outside the trailer waiting for the press conference to end. Sure enough, the trailer door opened, and out came Charlton Heston with a conga line of reporters and bodyguards following him. Once again I got at the end of the line. Charlton Heston is a very tall and handsome man. He takes big strides when he walks, and he was striding up the hill to his limo. David told me, "This is your last chance. If you're going to meet him, you better make it now!" My knees were weak. I was scared. Finally, I mustered up the nerve to yell, "Mr. Heston!" Unbelievably, he stopped dead in his tracks, turned, and looked at this little trembling figure with a cheap, Instamatic camera in her hands. Then, in that deep, Moses voice, he said, "Yes?"

I didn't know what to say as I approached this larger-than-life giant among stars. I looked him in the eyes and delivered my big line: "I loved you in *The Planet of the Apes*." He looked at me and a broad smile stretched across his handsome face, then he threw his head back and let out a deep laugh, the same laugh I had heard in the movies a million times. He extended his hand to me and told me to walk up the hill with him to his limousine. First I asked him if I could get my picture taken with him, and he agreed. I introduced him to David, they shook hands, and David took the picture. As I walked up the hill with Charlton Heston, I told him the shoe story. Once again he laughed heartily, then he told me he was sorry he had caused me inconvenience. He said he still orders his shoes from the same factory. When we reached the limo, he squeezed my hand and told me I was charming. Then I stood and watched as Moses drove out of my life.

In addition to the "Queen of Burlesque," I had another, more informal title: the "Marilyn Monroe of Times Square." I reminded people of Marilyn. When I walked down the streets of New York, some people would actually stop and stare. Passing construction sites had always been good for my ego, but at some point the men started adding something to their remarks: "Hey, Marilyn."

Now that I was out of burlesque, I was concentrating on my modeling. I set out to duplicate all the Marilyn Monroe shots that I had fallen in love with. The first would be the famous calendar nude shot, "Golden Dreams," by Tom Kelly, featuring a very young Norma Jean. I talked to several photographers about doing this particular shot. Each studied the photo, and all were a bit perplexed as to how exactly it had been done. Judging from the position of her body and how her breasts pointed straight out, I decided the photographer had to have been looking down at her. I tried the pose, but no photographer got it right. Their perspective was always off, resulting in things like my legs looking huge and my head looking tiny and far away. Usually the lighting was wrong, too.

Finally, I talked to another young photographer. He didn't have too much experience shooting models, or anything else for that matter, so he listened to my suggestions and respected my expertise in modeling. He didn't have the height in his studio to get up over me properly, so we had to find another location. At first a friend of his said we could come in one afternoon and do the shoot in his disco. He had a catwalk so my photographer could shoot straight down at me. This would be perfect. I went out and rented a huge, red velvet theater curtain, rings and all. One day before the shoot the photographer called me to say his "friend" had changed his mind, something to do with not wanting to get involved in porno.

"Now what?" I was frantic. As I racked my brain trying to come up with an idea, it hit me—the anteroom in my church! It had a very high ceiling. Why not? I asked our minister if we could do a shoot there. Of course, I didn't tell him it would be a nude session. I said it would be for a perfume ad. He said all right, but that we had to get done before four o'clock P.M. because that was when they would be holding a huge cake sale.

When we got there, all the tables were set up for the cakes. We locked the door and started shooting. It was the hottest day in July. I could feel my makeup melting. Thank goodness for the photographer's girlfriend. She kept dabbing my face with powder. Once I was in position I couldn't move, so she combed my hair out in ringlets for me, too. The photographer was so hot his sweat was dripping down on me. At one point there was a knock at the door. David got it. Two old ladies wanted to know if this was where the cake sale was being held. David very graciously got rid of them before they saw more than they bargained for.

The only baked goods on display were my buns.

We took two hundred shots before we called it a day. On the way home, we bought a bottle of pink champagne to celebrate. While we were walking into the house, I said to David, "I hope we got it this time. I wonder if Marilyn was watching. If only she could give me a sign that it turned out good." Suddenly, the bag with the pink champagne broke, and the bottle hit the curb with a crash! The cool, pink liquid trickled down the gutter in a foamy little stream. I believe Marilyn made her presence known that day. The next day the photographer called and told me to come over. We'd gotten it! It was the third picture out of the two hundred. I'm very proud of that shot. We display it over my television at home.

The next complicated Marilyn shot would be the shot from *Seven Year Itch*—Marilyn with the air from the subway grate blowing her white dress up around her hips. The twenty-fifth anniversary of Marilyn's death was coming up, and I wanted to do something special to remember her by. I wanted to do the shot on the exact same subway grate Marilyn had stood on. David got to work securing permission from the city. We had to rent a wind machine and have the white dress made. I found an excellent seamstress, Connie Gaggiano. She made me a replica of the dress from just the photo. David got all the permits in order and we were off.

The day of the shoot was cold, windy, and drizzling. My photographer, Annie Sprinkle, assured me it didn't matter. We had to get the sidewalks cleared, plus we had special traffic police to keep traffic moving. There were lots of people cheering me on, yelling "Marilyn! Marilyn!" Cars were stopping to watch, and people in stores on the other side of the street came out and started lining the sidewalks. It looked like they were waiting for a parade. This was one of the most exciting experiences I ever had. The wind blowing my skirt up felt wonderful. The adulation I experienced that day was nearly too much to handle. I felt like Marilyn herself, as if her spirit had taken me over.

As I sat bundled up in the limo on the way home, I couldn't help wondering what it must have been like to actually be Marilyn, if this was how she had been treated. It's as if people don't want to believe she's dead. They wanted me to be her. One young man leaned over the sawhorses and said to me, "I thought you were dead." Someone asked me about the Kennedys. They looked to me for answers I couldn't possibly have. They tried to touch my dress and hair. As we drove away they waved. "Goodbye, Marilyn." I loved it, but it was a little weird.

August 1987 was the twenty-fifth anniversary of Marilyn's death. They were running her films on television and planning various specials dedicated to the Sex Goddess. One day my friend Barbara Mazziotti told me she had seen a bunch of Marilyn Monroe lookalikes the night before on the "Joe Franklin Show." She thought it was too bad I hadn't been on the show. Barbara had also heard that there was going to be a big Marilyn Monroe lookalike contest coming up, but she wasn't sure when or where. I was frantic. What better way to pay tribute to Marilyn Monroe? How could I get in on the contest? Could I hold my own with other Marilyns? I had to find out. I wasn't going into the contest with winning on my mind. That would be too much to hope for, but being able to say I had been in the running would be good enough for me. It would be fun, too. I called the television station to see if I could get more information on the contest. A secretary told me to call a New York number, and I did. I expected to get a frizzy-haired little secretary, the "What's-this-in-reference-to" type. Instead, I got him—Joe Franklin! I heard that unmistakable voice talking to me. I told him my name was Yvette Paris, and he immediately cracked a joke. "No, no, Yvette," he said. I didn't get it, but he explained, "Like in the play, *No, No, Nanette*. Get it?" Sort of. This was a sense of humor one had to get used to. Little did I know I would have to. Joe told me how to get into the contest—it would be held the following weekend, and he would be one of the judges. All the judges had to have one qualification—they all had to have known the real Marilyn Monroe. This was going to be a big deal. What would I wear?

The morning of the contest my insides were shaking. I decided on the white dress I wore on the subway grate. Actually, it was my only Marilyn Monroe dress. There would be twenty-seven other contestants. I had a hell of a time gluing on my false eyelashes. When I finally got them on, I noticed in horror that they were on the wrong eyes! The contest was being held in the Grammercy Park Hotel in New York City. The first M.M. lookalike was very nice, only she was a he! The poor guy was dressed in the white blow-up dress, high heels, blond pin-up wig, and ruby-red lips. The only problem was that he also had five o'clock shadow! He showed me a tape recorder he brought with him. He was going to lipsync to "Diamonds Are a Girl's Best Friend."

Suddenly people were pushing and shoving. Someone very famous had just showed up, but I couldn't get near enough to see. Eventually the crowd thinned out, though, and I saw it was none other than Joe Franklin. I was so excited! I had to go up and ask to be photographed with him. He was so wonderful. Of course, I got my picture. I have that photograph hanging at home. I told Joe who I was, the "Queen of Burlesque," and said I wanted to go on his show to discuss the book I was writing on my life in burlesque. He was all for it. He said to call him.

The contest went by quickly, and, before I knew it, the time had come to choose the winner. I could hear all the other girls' hearts beating along with mine. First they called third runner-up, then second runner-up, then first runner-up: number five, Yvette Paris! I stood there like a zombie clapping along with everyone else, wondering who this girl was. A hand gave me a shove, and I shook out of it—"Oh shit," it was me! I was first runner-up! I couldn't believe it. I never expected to win anything, let alone second place! Wow! This was the greatest feeling yet.

Cameras flashed in our faces all day. All the winners had to go out in front of the hotel and pose for countless photographers. The winner and I were invited to the "Joe Franklin Show" to discuss the contest. Joe wanted to talk about my burlesque book, too. It would be my first on television—in America. (Once when I was a barmaid in the Yugoslavian-Albanian bar, the owner shot some film footage of the place to air on Radio Free Albania. Naturally, I never got to see it, but that was no big loss. All I did was stand in between the owner and his wife and wave stupidly at the camera.)

The "Joe Franklin Show" was wonderful. Joe is a great talk-show host, the best. He made us feel really at ease. Joe talked to me extensively about my book, and he made me look good. I'll always be grateful to Joe Franklin for giving me my first break on television.

As a child I watched "Joe Franklin's Memory Lane" with my mom. Mom was in love with Joe Franklin. Whatever she was doing came to a screeching halt when "Memory Lane" came on. She thought Joe was terribly handsome. I used to be jealous of Joe because he took my mother's attention away from me. I had the opportunity to visit the Memory Lane. It's not quite what I expected. I had visions of huge offices and a hundred secretaries to get through before you could get to Joe Franklin. In fact, Joe has a small office. It's covered with hundreds of old photos of the Hollywood of yesterday, as if Hollywood exploded and landed all over the office. There's a small couch among the clutter where you'll find Joe holding court. When the phone rings, the only way to find it is to pull the cord and wait for the phone to slide out from under something. Despite the clutter, Joe is a very sharp and organized man. Nothing gets by him. In a business where many people are eaten alive, Joe Franklin is a survivor. He's a legend in the business—when Joe talks, people listen—but he is also a true gentleman in a business that, for the most part, doesn't even know the meaning of the word.

For the twenty-fifth anniversary of M.M.'s death, I did a twelve-page calendar depicting some of M.M.'s more famous poses, along with renditions of the poses of two earlier sex goddesses, Jayne Mansfield and Jean Harlow. The Jean Harlow photos were done entirely in black and white, because they hadn't perfected colored film in the 1930s, and I wanted to be as true to her original image as possible. I did all the makeup for this calendar myself. When it came time to do Jean Harlow I used traditional silent-film makeup—a yellowish foundation and black lipstick. This gives the authentic look of the 1930s. Red lipstick photographs light in black and white, but black gives the silent-film vamp effect. I styled my own hair as well. I wore no wigs in the photos.

When I was finished being shot for the Jean Harlow photos, I was in a hurry and left the studio in full makeup. Fortunately, I was in New York City and went completely unnoticed.

David and I advertised the calendar in *Penthouse* and a few other men's magazines. I use them for promotions and for my fans. People still send in for the calendar, even though it's out of date. I understand that it's considered a collector's item now.

After I was on the "Joe Franklin Show" things started going very well for me. I got a call from another talk show, "People Are Talking," with host Richard Bey. The episode was going to be about exhibitionists. They wanted me to perform a mock strip. Along with me, they planned to have a Chippendale's male stripper, a *Penthouse* Pet, a television talk-show hostess for a nude show, a *Playgirl* model, and a stage performer from the long-running play *Oh! Calcutta.*

Then I was invited on "Best Talk in Town," with host Nola Roper. Once again, I was asked to perform a make-believe strip. I sent Nola into a fit of laughter just before the show started. I told her about an all-nude talk show where even the cameraman was nude, except for evening socks. When I told her to visualize her cameramen totally nude except for evening socks, she went berserk with laughter. It was hard for her to keep a straight face after the cameras started rolling.

Sally Jessy Raphael is one of the nicest ladies I have ever met. I was asked on her show to discuss burlesque along with such great stars as Ann Corio, Dixie Evans, Bambi Vawn, and Jennie Lee. The producers treated us like royalty, but then we *were* all Burlesque Queens. A big black limousine came to take me to the show in Connecticut. The best part of the show was meeting Ann Corio, a woman who is synonymous with burlesque. She was very open and friendly. I told her a story about my father. One day, when he was working for Western Union, he had had to deliver a telegram to a "Miss Ann Corio." She was only sixteen years old, but she was already considered the Queen of Burlesque. Well, he thought she was the most beautiful creature he had ever seen. For years to come Pop would talk about seeing Ann Corio. Once my mother had enough of it and whacked him with a pot. When Annie heard that story she laughed so hard she had tears in her eyes. I got to ride home in the limousine with Ann. The driver surprised us with a bottle of cold champagne. I became friends with Ann Corio, and she told me plenty about being a good stripper. A direct quote from Ann: "A man's imagination is a woman's biggest asset."

I went to see Annie's fantastic "This Was Burlesque" show three times when she brought it to New York. It was my last chance to get to see how it really was. The most exciting part, of course, was Ann doing her striptease. The audience fell silent as she paraded down the runway twirling her famous parasol. She seduced the whole audience with her little-girl voice and ultra-long eyelashes. She was sensational—and she never had to take it off.

When I went to receive my Golden Fanny Award in the summer of 1989, Ann came with me for moral support. She was dressed immaculately. She even had on white afternoon tea gloves. The press was there and snapping photos of us galore. Someone suggested that we take our tops off for a sexy shot. Jeez! Talk about no class. Ann leaned over to me and whispered in my ear, "If you take your top off, I'll slap you one." Of course, I had no such intention, but I sure wouldn't want to get Annie mad. She looks like she has one hot Italian temper.

Ann Corio was my teacher, but the rest was up to me. I studied Annie's movements and her ladylike style. It paid off for me. Although I had to take off all my clothes for today's audiences, I did it with style and grace. I teased, something that is almost unheard of today.

Also on the "Sally Jessy Raphael Show" was the Marilyn Monroe of burlesque, the great Dixie Evans. Dixie was the twin of Marilyn Monroe when Marilyn was at her peak. She looked so much like the star that *Photoplay* magazine wrote, "Marilyn Monroe Vexed over Stripper Dixie Evans." Marilyn's lawyer even sued Dixie for looking too much like her. Dixie and I became fast friends and she taught me plenty about burlesque.

I was probably the most thrilled to meet Jennie Lee. Not enough can be said about this feisty stripper. She's the girl Jan and Dean wrote their first hit about—"Jennie Lee." In the late 1950s they saw a big poster of her outside a burlesque theater and fell in love with the mysterious "Bazoom Girl," so they immortalized her in song. Jennie Lee is founder of the "Stripper Hall of Fame" in Helendale, California. I was recently inducted into the Stripper Hall of Fame and awarded the Golden Fanny Award by none other than Jennie Lee herself. The Golden Fanny Award is an award given to strippers who do humane deeds.* The award is a plaque with the shape of Jennie Lee's rear end on it. In the exotic world, this is the equivalent of an Oscar.

We talked up a storm on the "Sally Jessy Raphael Show," and when we got out of the building there were three shiny, stretch limos waiting for us. Dixie's was white, Jennie Lee's was gold, and Annie and I had a black one. They looked pretty impressive all lined up.

For his fortieth birthday I wanted to give David something different, so I set up a photo shoot with my dear friend Annie Sprinkle, a world-famous porno star as well as a top-notch photographer. She photographed us for an adult magazine in various sexual poses. Then we posed for several other sex magazines. A few weeks later we even filled in for a couple in a porno movie who didn't want to have sex due to the AIDS scare. You never saw our faces, only my lips and David's cock. This stuff keeps our love life exciting. This is not to tell the average couple to go out and pose for sex magazines— just to be sexy for each other.

---

*Yvette Paris sponsors two foster children in Columbia and one in the Philippines. During the Christmas and Easter holiday seasons, she volunteers at St. Mary's Church, making up food boxes for underprivileged families. She is a member of the Make-a-Wish Foundation, which fulfills wishes, in the form of gifts, of children with terminal diseases. She also sponsors Sonny the Elephant at her local Humane Society and donates to other Humane Societies.

I'm happy posing for men's magazines—sixty spreads so far and counting. I like dealing with the people of the exotic world. I am also a contributing editor to *D-Cup* magazine. My dear friend Bob Rosen, editor of *D-Cup*, gave me that status. *D-Cup* is a magazine that prints voluptuous women with D-cup bra sizes. I'm a 38D. I met Bob through Neil Wexler, editor of *Adults Only* magazine, who did an excellent story on me.

Bob is one of the few men's magazine editors who ever took me seriously. He always gave me great coverage. He gave me the first cover shot I could be really proud of. I'm very popular with *D-Cup* readers. Because of *D-Cup,* I have a large fan club now.

Bob was watching a horror movie once, a splatter-type movie, when, to his surprise, a guy sitting on the toilet in one scene turned out to be jerking off to an issue of *D-Cup.* And of all the lovely girls in that issue, this actor had it opened to a large spread on "Yvette Paris." When Bob called me up and told me the story, I almost died laughing. Well, I had finally gotten onto the silver screen.

I have a large fan club created by the men's magazines I have posed for. I get mail from all over the United States, and all over the world, including Japan, Poland, Canada, England, France, and Germany. Many of my fans are prisoners. I get mail from Attica, even Leavenworth. The prisoners usually write me the nicest letters. Many propose marriage to me. I guess they figure they have nothing to lose. Many share their personal problems with me and actually ask me for advice. I write back to all my fans and send them photos.

I was so popular with the inmates at one prison that I was voted their "Prison Playmate of the Year." They even wrote about me in their newspaper. I don't take lightly the fact that these men are in the can for a very good reason. They never tell me just what exactly they are in for, and I never ask. I only see very lonely individuals reaching out for someone to talk to. If that is all they want, then I can take the time to listen. These men will eventually be released, and I would rather have them released with the attitude that someone cares than with the attitude that the whole world stinks.

Not all my fans are prisoners, however. Doctors, lawyers, even scientists write to me. I rarely get a letter from a crackpot or a pervert. Some teenage boys write to me claiming to be "sexperts" and telling me that what I really need is a man. I tell them, "Thanks, but no thanks. I have a couple like you at home."

Recently, out of the blue, I received a letter from my brother, Jack. He dropped a bomb on me. He said that I was pornographic, that I do not resemble any sister of his, that I am not to write or contact him in any way, and that I am to keep to my own family and he will keep to his. Jack said fellow police officers would come up to him with magazines with me in them and say, "Is this your sister?" Then they would make sexual remarks. My brother was ashamed. Little did Jack know that when I was go-go dancing, I often ran into a number of his so-called friends. They told me about a lot of wild and embarrassing things my brother did when he got loaded. Still, I never criticized him. It didn't affect me at all. Besides, what kind of friends were they anyway, to tell me all those things?

My brother and I were always very close. Narrow-minded and self-righteous religiousness is responsible for this unnecessary break between us. He knows the real me, yet he chooses to be swayed by stupid ideas and piggish friends. So be it. I remain very proud of all his accomplishments. He is a highly decorated police officer who has saved many lives and gallantly delivered a number of babies in the line of duty.

In less open ways my aunts, uncles, and cousins act much like Jack. They are nonexistent to me. I've had better conversations with bums on street corners in New York. I'm a stupid person—I keep trying to hold family and friends together, but every time I come out in a new magazine or on a TV show discussing stripping, they make the sign of the cross and run for their lives. Wives hold onto their husbands for dear life, as though I want their damn husbands. Children are sheltered from me, as if I'd change their daughters into hookers or porno stars and their sons into Chippendale dancers. What goes through their minds? People who don't know me like me instantly. I get along with everybody. There is no class system as far as I am concerned. I like all types of people. My mother once said, "If a flying saucer ever lands, my daughter will be the first to make friends with the aliens."

Today

I'm making private striptease videos that I sell through mail order. David has a successful mail-order business. Jimmy is planning to marry soon. Jack is playing bass in a heavy metal band. Juliet is an orange belt in jujitsu and studies guitar. We are all very happy.

Private Dancer

In my time as a stripper, I got to ask a lot of men why they came to strip shows. Why weren't they home with their wives? I got some pretty interesting answers. Most of them loved their wives, but felt they weren't interested in sex or being sexy. So, ladies, as the old saying goes, "Keep him well fed at home and he won't have to eat out." Don't fool yourself into thinking your man is too old, or too anything else, to be interested in sex. Men are very sexual by nature—never too preoccupied and definitely never too old to want sex to be an important part of their lives. You'd be surprised at the oldies in burlesque theaters still chasing the young strippers—and catching them sometimes, by the way.

It's common knowledge that many women fantasize about being strippers, taking it all off for a room full of men. Alas, most women only fantasize. Well, ladies, I can tell you how to perform a strip act for your husband, really turn him on, fulfill your stripper fantasy, and just plain have fun.

First wait until the kids are asleep. Exchange white light bulbs in the bedroom lamp for sexy red. Buy satin sheets and prop your husband up on the bed with a chilled glass of champagne. Get soft, sexy music to play on your tape player (no rock music, please). Now put on sexy panties, preferably black or red lace. Buy a garter belt. Men love them. Get black or black fishnet stockings. Buy a black or red push-up bra. Now put on a gown or a long, fancy nightgown. Do your hair and put on sexy, whory-looking makeup and long earrings. Try to get a feather boa. Costume stores sell them. If possible, get long opera gloves.

Now for your strip. Slowly twirl to the music for a while. Start by dropping your boa (on your husband). Next, slowly remove your gloves. Then slowly unzip your gown. Please don't pull it over your head—slip out of it. Now remove your bra, then the garter belt, then the stockings, and last of all the panties. Fade to black.

This will work with 98 percent of all husbands. Of course, there's still the 2 percent of men who will run around on their wives no matter what. Short of divorce, I don't know what to tell you, ladies.

Don't think you have to be a ravishing beauty or even slim to do a strip act. God knows the dancers at the burlesque theaters aren't all slim. You need only be willing to have fun with the man you love. If you do, why should he go out to a burlesque theater? He can keep his eyes on you!